BRIGHTSEA

BRIGHTSEA

JANE GILLESPIE

St. Martin's Press
New York

Library of Congress Cataloging-in-Publication Data

Gillespie, Jane, 1932-
    Brightsea.

    I. Title.
PR6057.I574B7   1987   823'.914   86-26213
ISBN 0-312-00111-8

First published in Great Britain by Robert Hale Limited.

First Edition

10 9 8 7 6 5 4 3 2 1

1

Nature had endowed Miss Steele with good health, lively spirits and an optimistic outlook; of which last she stood in some need, since nature had omitted to endow her with beauty, brains or sensibility. Nor were her worldly circumstances more propitious; her father was in a small way of business in Devon which could yield her no fortune, and she had been given very little in the way of education. She had now passed her fortieth birthday, but her optimism still kept her hopeful of acquiring a husband.

Her immediate family was not extensive; she had one sister, seven years younger than herself. Their mother had died early and their father devoted himself only to his business. The Miss Steeles soon recognised that they must make their own way in the world, and passed most of their time in visiting cousins and friends, who received them the more willingly as the young ladies learned to make their way by obliging and flattering manners, whatever their deficiencies in taste or delicacy. The younger Miss Steele, endowed with more beauty, quickness and guile than her sister, succeeded in making a marriage far above her apparent deserving, to a gentleman with estates in Norfolk and a house in London. To this household Miss Steele, after the death of her father, attached herself with every expectation of finding as suitable a partner. As the years passed, however, her sister became increasingly preoccupied with her own domestic concerns; she quarrelled with her husband, bullied her children, and above all strove to remain on good terms with her husband's fine relations, whose good opinion she valued and whose manners she learned to imitate. Miss Steele, satisfied with her own manners and desirous of more attention, from time to time absented herself on visits to former friends to give herself a change of scene and company and to show off her new gowns. She would have been incredulous had she been told that some of her wider family circle accepted her from pity.

This was not the case with her cousin Mrs Palmer in Cleveland, whose own nature was so happy that she could conceive of no unhappiness in anyone else, nor of anything but enjoyment from any event. When she received, on a dull winter morning, a letter from Miss Steele, she had scarcely read it before she ran with it to her husband's writing-room.

"Oh, Mr Palmer, here is delightful news: I have a letter from – wait – from Nancy and she is coming to visit us. I have not seen her for as long as I remember."

"Your memory is short," observed Mr Palmer without raising his eyes from his pen. "They visited us in Berkeley Street shortly before Christmas."

"Yes, I am sure they did. Where should I be, without your cleverness to remind me of such things?"

"Lost in stupidity," suggested her husband.

Mrs Palmer laughed merrily at the suggestion. It was Mr Palmer's habit to employ incivility as a means of displaying his wit and dignity, a practice which his wife's pleasure in his utterances did nothing to discourage. "To be sure, I should. But you will wish to hear what Nancy writes." Although Mr Palmer continued to write, she read aloud:

"My dear Charlotte: London is amazing dull now and I expect you are glad to be away from it. Lucy did not take me to the Rolands' party on Thursday, I suppose she thought Mr Bruce would be there, but I do not care for him at all. The new colour now is pink but this town air makes my complexion not fit for it. I will come to you for a week or two because Lucy and me are not speaking but I suppose she will give me money for travelling, to be rid of me. I do not want to go to Delaford in spite of they asked me. You know how sober they all are, but the country is so dull in winter. Cleveland is better because it is so near to Bristol so I expect there will be balls and society. You can perhaps send to meet me in Bristol on next Friday. Yours ...' My dear Mr Palmer," added Mrs Palmer folding the letter, "you will be in Bristol next Friday, will you not, on business, so you can conveniently bring her here?"

"Bring whom?" inquired Mr Palmer, looking back over his own letter.

"Oh, how absurd you are; I declare, you did not listen to a word I said! Your drollery will be the death of me."

Her husband gave her a sombre glance implying that such an outcome was too much to hope for. He had heard quite well, indeed, and now relented so far as to say:

"It will not be at all convenient to hang about the coaching station in quest of Miss Steele, whom I shall doubtless miss because she has fallen in with some unlucky companion and thrust herself into his post-chaise. She will arrive here before me and thrust herself upon *us* for her usual interminable visit. Were she to wait for herself to be invited here, her company would be more tolerable."

"But you never find her company tolerable, my dear. Though I know you are fond of her in your quiet way. So am I, very fond of Nancy, though she will talk all the time about herself until I am wearied of her before she has been a half-hour in the house. She is a good simple creature, in spite of her affected manner, and she trims herself such ridiculous bonnets, but always makes them so pretty, I cannot help admiring her taste, hideous as her style is. And she will bring the children sweets and presents, they become spoilt at once and I can do nothing with them while she is with us —"

"You can do little with them when she is not with us," remarked Mr Palmer. "They have been doted on until they are quite out of hand."

"How can you say so? You know quite well that they are fine, lively little beings and you admire their spirit. Well," as Mr Palmer did not condescend to contradict this, "I shall be glad to have Nancy here. She will be someone for me to talk to, when she is not talking herself, and country air will improve her complexion, not that she stirs out of doors at this time of the year, and she always cheers me up, except that she complains all the time of Lucy and that family; but she will give us news of them, if one can believe all she says, and I am looking forward already to her arrival."

"And I," said Mr Palmer, "to her departure."

Mrs Palmer, laughing heartily at that, went off to reply to Miss Steele's letter in the friendliest terms, serenely confident that Mr Palmer would arrange to convey Miss Steele from Bristol to Cleveland and entertain her with his charming witticisms for as long as she chose to remain with them. Everyone would have a happy time.

Everyone appeared to. Miss Steele never suspected herself unwelcome, provided as she was with sweetmeats for the children and gossip for Mrs Palmer. She stood in some awe of Mr Palmer's grave demeanour, ascribing it to his cleverness and hence, knowing herself not clever, not troubling to understand his few speeches to herself and so taking no offence at them. She laughed with Mrs Palmer when Mr Palmer said:

"I believe you are come because your sister is tired of you."

"Oh, my dear," his wife answered him, "you know that Nancy and Lucy are as close as sisters can be, even when they are not speaking!"

"I dare say that would make for greater closeness."

"Is he not a tease, Nancy?"

Miss Steele readily agreed. Attention from Mr Palmer she accepted as flattering, without feeling equipped to reply to it. While she was alone with Mrs Palmer she had more to say about her relations with her sister.

"I promise you, Charlotte, Lucy has been out of humour these many weeks. What she needs to be so cross about, I cannot see. Of course, she has the children always being naughty, and that terrible mother-in-law to please. It may be she envies me my lack of attachments – permanent ones, I mean. She snaps my head off as soon as I mention any of my beaux." About these, Miss Steele welcomed any amount of teasing. "She refused to lend me her garnet necklace, simply because she said it did not match with my pink gown, but indeed they went very prettily together, and I am sure I would lend her anything of mine that she wanted. She pretends I have no taste, but I have more experience than she, of choosing clothes – Depend on it, she was afraid I was wishing to make an impression on Mr Bruce, but who would care to impress such a silly smirking creature? He has taken up with some girl from Camberwell who has freckles on her face, and I wish him joy of her. There is no one in town worth meeting nowadays. And Lucy would not give me nearly enough money for my journey, although I promised to pay her back, as soon as I have saved: as it was, I owe six shillings to the milliner, since I had trimmed up my best bonnet so often it fell to pieces, and I had to have a new muff and boots, for the country – Lord knows when I shall pay for those. Lucy knows I have so little of my own, yet she complains all the time that she is short of money – Of course, Robert is so extravagant, and heavens, how they quarrel about that. You can hear them screaming at each other from one end of the house to the other. But his mother is rich, and they have the Norfolk property – I do not know why Robert cannot sell some of his horses, or farms, but when I offer any advice, I am accused of interfering and my head is snapped off again. Lord, money is a difficulty, is it not?"

Mrs Palmer consoled her: "Oh, Nancy, money is not important, provided of course one does not need to buy anything. Mr Palmer pretends to be angry with me because I spend so much on the housekeeping, but he pays the bills and we go on as usual. I am sure Lucy will pay your milliner as soon as you are friends again, and indeed while you are living with her you have free lodging and she is glad to have you, and she need not seriously think of money. She must keep a sharp eye on it nevertheless, because I believe Robert is fond of gaming and is a coxcomb, but he means no harm, and with Lucy to guide him and his mother behind him he can surely afford to be liberal towards yourself? Although he has not a generous nature I hear; and Lucy can be irritable, but then Robert must be provoking at times: not all husbands are as easy as Mr Palmer. You are fortunate perhaps to remain single."

"I have chosen to remain so," returned Miss Steele nettled, "on account of some of the examples of unhappy marriages I have seen. I have had as many chances of marriage, I am sure, as anyone; but it does not do, to rush into such things."

"No, indeed. Lucy and her husband made a runaway marriage, did they not? But yet, they have settled very well together. I am sorry they quarrel so much. Well, we shall go to the ball given by the Watsons in Bristol – except, I seem to remember, they are in Scotland until the summer – In any event, we shall find some way of entertaining you, and you must stay a long while – Unless Mr Palmer decides to go to London, which he recently spoke of – And I declare, you will see no example of an unhappy marriage while you are with *us*," asserted Mrs Palmer in great contentment. She offered to lend Miss Steele enough money to repay her immediate debts to Lucy, an offer which Miss Steele accepted with token protest. This item of expenditure, when Mr Palmer perceived it in his wife's accountings, brought from him a comment that no one but Mrs Palmer would have dared to find amusing.

The money was sent to Lucy but no acknowledgement returned. More than three weeks passed, during which Mrs Palmer was merry, Mr Palmer increasingly morose, and the children increasingly insolent under the injudicious attentions of the visitor. When the eldest boy threw snowballs at Miss Steele and ruined her second best bonnet, he and his mother were the only ones to enjoy the comedy. Miss Steele began to wonder whether Lucy was gone into Norfolk, or whether the money and its accompanying propitiatory letter had gone astray, or even whether Lucy intended to cut her off altogether. Mr Palmer said to his wife: "I begin to wonder whether we are to have her with us for ever." Mrs Palmer's laughter at such a notion was perhaps not as wholehearted as usual.

2

Spring was now approaching and Mr and Mrs Palmer did wish to pass some time in their London house. "Must we," inquired Mr Palmer, "take Miss Steele with us?"

"I do not suppose so. But, I see no other course. She cannot go back to Lucy if they are still not speaking. Though, I am sure she could, and they would very soon forgive each other. Or might she go to her cousins in Holborn? The trouble is, that everywhere in town she will meet the same people as Lucy, and I do not expect she will like to be asked why they have quarrelled. That is, if they have."

"Their quarrels need not concern us."

"Certainly they need not. Quarrels between sisters are so unnecessary, unless there is some serious necessity. You remember that, after Mama died, when we knew she had left me the Berkeley Street house, Mary was ready to quarrel with me about it, although she had a far finer house of her own in town. I simply laughed at her."

Mr Palmer, not attending, mused: "Our problem remains: We must somehow dispose of Miss Steele."

"My dear Mr Palmer, how can you speak in that way, when she is a cousin and I am so fond of her? I knew you would say some whimsical thing like that. Yes, what is to be done with her?"

By chance, on the very next day, it was Mr Palmer who was able to put forward a solution to their problem. Being in Bristol on business he visited, as he often did, an elderly gentleman who had been a friend of his late father and who lived a solitary invalid's life. Infirm as Mr Retford was, he had survived his wife and two children. Ill-health was believed to run in the family. At this time, the only relative left to him was a granddaughter, still a child and at school.

It was about this granddaughter that Mr Retford complained today, even more fretfully than about his aching head, the east winds, his doctors' neglect and the price of candles. Mr Palmer was accustomed to listening to such complaints with a patience that would have surprised many of his friends. Alone with Mr Retford he felt no demands on his wit or dignity and could be quietly sympathetic. It appeared that Mr Retford was indeed in a difficulty.

The story was: Louisa was now sixteen years old and of an age to leave school. Hitherto, her holidays from school had been passed anywhere than under her grandfather's roof; fond as he was of her, Mr Retford had never been strong enough to support the idea of someone running up and down stairs, playing a pianoforte, bringing in friends who would chatter and laugh; he knew what was due to the child and was wealthy to provide it, at a distance from himself. He explained to Mr Palmer that the doctors had not been satisfied with Louisa's health of late, and had recommended sea air. Very well; a house had been taken at Brightsea, servants sent down to prepare it, and Louisa's governess summoned to accompany her. "It was all arranged," said Mr Retford plaintively, stretching his hands to the fire. "Ring for more coal, will you? I can *not* shake off this chill, and the sudden perplexity does not help me. It was all arranged, but then her governess writes to tell me she must go abroad. Her sister has to live in a warmer climate and apparently only Miss Worthington can escort her. That may be so, but what is to be done? She gives no thought to my own situation. Louisa must have a companion. She does not require a governess now, of course. There is nothing Miss Worthington could teach her now. In truth, Louisa is a bookish little thing, and should be encouraged to take fresh air, and I suppose, at her age, to go into society? I do not know. I do not know at all what should be done with a girl of that age. It is all too much for me. I suffer severely from this weather. In only three days from now Louisa leaves the school. I cannot have her here. My nerves would give way completely."

Shaking his head in suitable alarm at such a prospect, Mr Palmer said: "Surely, another companion could be found? The house, you say, has been taken for only the summer? There must be many respectable ladies who would be glad of such a position –" He broke off, recollecting that he might have such a candidate under his own roof.

He promised Mr Retford nothing definite, but returned home determined to persuade Miss Steele of her eligibility for the post of companion to Miss Retford. At the dinner-table, he discovered that Miss Steele saw the question rather the other way about.

"But, Mr Palmer, I am not sunk so low that I must take paid employment."

"I do not think the employment would be onerous."

"But I have never thought of myself as a mere governess."

Avoiding the observation that Miss Steele was hardly qualified to be a governess at all, however mere, he said: "No teaching duties would be required. The girl is, I am sure, well behaved, and the house will be well appointed."

Mrs Palmer had from its first mention thought the whole idea the most delightful in the world, and now struck in:

"With servants, Nancy. Imagine that. And Brightsea –
There will be all kinds of gay doings during the summer in
such a place. I wonder you can hesitate for a moment.
Besides, Mr Retford is very rich, is he not, Mr Palmer? I
am sure you will be able to order what you like for the table
with no thought of expense. I dare say he even expects to
provide a carriage for Miss Retford. Why, you would be
living in more luxury than even Lucy,'' she added, artlessly.

At that, the plan began to recommend itself to Miss Steele.
After so long a breach from Lucy, pride would not tolerate a
renewed approach; if the girl were docile, and the servants
well trained, the companion's duties might be nominal. It
would be a great joke, to write to Lucy from a fashionable
address, describing a life of luxury and exhibiting
independence. And who knew whom one might meet, in the
society of a famous watering place such as Brightsea?
Besides, Mr Retford would be obliged to pay his
granddaughter's chaperone on the scale of his reputed
wealth; there could be new gowns, even a necklace to replace
the ambers she had rashly given to Lucy for her birthday.
And, Miss Steele reminded herself, she need not stay in
Brightsea longer than she liked it; if she did not like it, she
had many friends to go to; which reminded her further:

"Charlotte, if when you go to town you see Lucy, or any
of those others – if you are writing to the Brandons, or meet
with the Middletons – as a favour, tell them I am gone to
some *friends* in Brightsea. I will explain in my own good
time, if I stay there, about me taking a kind of situation.
There can be no harm in having them think I have made
new friends of my own.''

"Oh, yes, I will not tell anyone anything, unless they ask
me, and then I shall not say a word, I promise you.''

Mr Palmer withheld a comment on his wife's discretion,
in his anxiety that Miss Steele should not be deterred from
her venture. Miss Steele was now lamenting only the
shortness of the time left to her for her preparations:

"Lord, I must be there in three days from now, and I

have not a thing ready. I wish you could have Betty mend
the rent in my spotted muslin, and the fringe is worn on my
blue shawl. I shall not be fit to be seen. Charlotte, if you
would lend my your tippet ..."

The haste necessary to the arrangements may have
worked, did Miss Steele but know it, to her advantage. Mr
Retford, complain as he did about the inadequacies of his
domestic staff, possessed in his housekeeper, Mrs Collier, a
woman of sense and responsibility. She had taken pains in
the choice of the servants for the house in Brightsea and
overseen the setting up of the household there. On the
defection of Miss Worthington, however, she had no time to
select a new companion for Miss Retford, but had to rely on
the recommendation of her employer's friend Mr Palmer.
There could be a doubt that she would have considered
Miss Steele altogether suitable, especially had she seen Miss
Steele arrayed in the style that Miss Steele herself thought
suitable to her new status and duties. Miss Steele decided
that, as companion to a young girl, she should appear
youthful; and that, lest she be taken for one in a servile
position, she must appear elegant. Tricked up in the finest of
her wardrobe, augmented by several items of Mrs
Palmer's, she travelled straight to Brightsea. Miss Retford
travelled there from her school, whither her grandfather
had sent a servant for her, and it was in the Brightsea house
that she and Miss Steele confronted each other. On each
side there was at this first meeting some slight misgiving.

The house itself had delighted Miss Steele on her arrival.
It was in a modern crescent, set a little back from the
sea-front, and in excellent order. Fingering the silk of the
curtains, Miss Steele could not calculate how many ball
gowns might have been made from them and at what cost.
The servants had received her deferentially; there were, it
seemed, two maids and a man; the upper maid, curtseying,
had asked: "Which bedroom would you wish to have,
ma'am?" and Miss Steele had inspected four, charmingly
decorated, before selecting the front, above the drawing-

room. She had had time to do no more than this before Miss Retford was due to arrive, so she hastily curled up her hair and posed herself on the sofa in her best violet-ribboned dress and beaded shawl, her embroidery frame to hand. Very soon there was the sound of a carriage outside.

Miss Steele remained where she was. It would make a false first impression if she were to go down to meet the young lady; let the young lady be presented, as it were, to the mistress of the house. Nevertheless Miss Steele's needle pricked her finger as she heard voices below. She told herself resolutely: The girl may be rich and educated and well connected but it's me has the authority here and I shall show her so, from the start.

"Miss Retford, ma'am," announced the manservant.

Miss Steele raised her eyes to behold a short, ill-dressed, dull-faced young girl entering the room, standing there with nothing to say for herself. For a long moment they regarded one another before the girl dropped her eyes and said: "How do you do."

Miss Steele omitted to answer, in her surprise that was between disappointment and relief. Lord, the creature was not even elegant. She wore a close bonnet and grey cape, with no jewellery, and was plumpish and pale. Miss Steele pursued her thought: I did expect her to have some air of fashion about her. What a mousy little thing. She will bore me to distraction. I shall go back to Cleveland – Though, to think of it, she may give little trouble, and if she is supposed to be in poor health, she does not appear delicate. I dare say I shall enjoy myself here in spite of her, so I may as well give it a chance. I need not have troubled with these violet ribbons.

Having concluded, these reflections Miss Steele said:

"You understand, I am here to be your companion, and not any sort of a governess. I came in a great hurry, to oblige your grandfather, whose friend is my cousin. I have not taken any sort of situation before, having not needed to, and indeed I do not need to now, but am in the way of obliging, so you and me will have to get along together and make the best of it, do you see?"

"Yes, ma'am," replied Miss Retford without raising her eyes. Miss Steele supposed her suitably warned. And so she was.

Louisa Retford had received with some trepidation the news that Miss Worthington would be unable to accompany her to Brightsea and that a strange Miss Steele was to take Miss Worthington's place. Louisa fully understood that in any case Miss Worthington's function as governess was now considered to be terminated. A new phase of Louisa's life was to begin, and this she viewed with no less trepidation.

Hitherto, her school holidays had been happily passed with Miss Worthington in lodgings; they had read, walked, passed some of the time with music and water-colour painting, but Louisa's grandfather had been exact in describing her as 'bookish'; she was naturally studious, and Miss Worthington, who had taught her until she went to school, had encouraged her in that. But, now, a house had been taken for Louisa, as if she were to be set up in an establishment. She understood that she was expected to come out into society, a prospect that afforded her both mild alarm and private vexation. She wished to be left to carry on her studies and was sure Miss Worthington would have permitted her to do so. She was perceptive enough to anticipate no such encouragement from Miss Steele in her finery on the sofa of this strange and fine drawing-room.

Louisa did not remember her parents. Books had soon offered her her only refuge from loneliness. At school, she had made few friends but no enemies; she had been allowed, being 'clever', to stand aloof. She did not regret leaving her school, which had by now no more to teach her; but, on the threshold of a quite unknown new life, she was at a loss. Trepidation did not entirely overwhelm her; she was used to making her own quiet decisions. Besides, she was used to being obedient and was well mannered. Postponing decision on Miss Steele, she still waited calmly on events.

"Well then," conceded Miss Steele, mollified by the girl's submissive politeness, "I dare say you are tired from the journey and would like some tea. I will tell the servants." She was rising in a flurry of frills, ready to open the drawing-room door and call down the stairs, when Miss Retford agreed:

"Thank you, ma'am. I should like some tea. Shall I ring the bell for you?" She crossed to the hearth and did so.

"Lord," remarked Miss Steele, unguarded, "I had forgot, one rings the bell in a house of this kind. – So they do," she retrieved herself, "in my sister's house in London, which is very grand. Larger than this house, I promise you."

Louisa could summon no answer to this, but asked instead whether she might withdraw to remove her travelling clothes? Irritated, Miss Steele cried:

"Bless me, you do not need ask my permission to take your bonnet off!" She began to think Miss Retford would prove too tame altogether. As they drank tea, Miss Steele entertained herself with an account of a ball at Lady Middleton's, but Miss Retford was not conspicuously entertained; of course, Miss Steele reflected, the girl would not have been to any balls yet herself, and so such tales of high life would fail to impress her. Disheartened after a while, Miss Steele announced that they were both tired from travel and would go early to bed.

3

Awakening to the seaside sunlight of a March morning, Miss Steele was much refreshed and in her most optimistic spirits, eager to view her new territory. "As soon as we have breakfasted," she told Miss Retford," we shall go out and have a look round Brightsea."

"Certainly, ma'am."

Brightsea was, at this stage of its history, fashionable because people of fashion had begun to find the more popular coastal resorts too crowded, and to seek a more select milieu. Hence many of Brightsea's buildings were still of recent construction and the effect was fresh and clean. Besides sea bathing, the town offered the waters of a mineral spring; there was a concert hall and a public ballroom. Miss Steele was delighted with all she saw. Pausing along the main shopping arcade she exclaimed: "Upon my soul, the shops here are as splendid as Bond Street!" That she had money to spend in such shops was a novelty to her, and it was unlikely that she would not enjoy the novelty to the full; optimism such as hers can conceive of no needy future. Mr Retford's remuneration was above anything she had been used to; she wondered in passing that she had not long ago thought of taking a situation, and even imagined that she might buy a small present to send to Charlotte Palmer for the loan of her tippet; her exhilaration almost led her to imagine that, if she could bear the company of this dull girl for long enough, she might buy a tippet for herself.

Such agreeable thoughts occupied a considerable time, and it was not until Louisa had paused to gaze into the window of a bookshop that Miss Steele recollected: "But we have not yet seen the sea! There must be somewhere to walk beside the sea. Hurry, while the sun shines. I wish I had my veil, because the sea air is supposed to harm the complexion, but no matter, I shall buy some rosewater lotion later –" And she led Louisa away from the shops, making for the sea-front, following a group of strollers whose ladies carried parasols. I must buy myself a parasol, Miss Steele noted; a pink one for instance would cast a flattering shade on my face.

They discovered a very pleasant promenade beside the

sea-shore, and discovered too that it seemed everyone walked to and fro here. Miss Steele and Louisa walked to and fro, Miss Steele from long habit scrutinising the dress of every lady, and the face of every gentleman, that she passed. This pursuit was almost as engrossing as her study of the shops. "Upon my word," she remarked, "the ladies here are all fearful fashionable, but I can't say I notice the men very handsome. It may be we shall have to go to a public ball to meet the beaux of Brightsea." As she spoke, a gentleman approached whose face commanded her attention. He was young, with a haughty profile and stylish dress, and he was walking alone. Miss Steele directed at him her most charming smile but he stared through her with an indifference amounting to insolence. She was not unaccustomed to such a reception of her charm, and said only: "Some people have no manners, I declare. If we pass that same horrid creature on our way back, be sure not to notice him." Louisa who had not noticed him in any case made no reply. Whereupon it occurred to Miss Steele: It is because I am forced to walk with this drab girl that no one admires me. Heavens, one might suppose *I* was walking with my governess. "We must buy you some new clothes," she added aloud. "I dare say your grandfather has given you money?"

"Yes, ma'am, but I do not care about what I wear."

"Anyone can see that. I expect your bonnet is the one you wore at school. Well, tomorrow we shall go to a good milliner, and then we shall have your hair decently styled, and you will look less of a fright."

Another handsome man was now coming towards them, and although he was only a clergyman, and was wheeling a Bath chair in which lay a thin white-faced lady, Miss Steele bestowed on him her smile. He returned a courteous nod. "Now *he* has not a bad phiz," commented Miss Steele. "Lord, my feet are tired. We'll sit a while on this seat, and quiz the people as they go by. See, a girl with a green parasol – it makes her look seasick. I wager that is her brother with

her. She is too shocking ugly to have a beau. Help me pull
forward the feathers of my bonnet, to shade my face from
the sun; it is hotter than I thought. Here comes that horrid
– No, it is not him." It was another solitary man, who
passed without glancing towards the ladies on the seat. "I
dare say we had better walk again. It does not do, to make
oneself singular by being out of things." But her feet still
ached and she let herself rest for a little. Meanwhile the
clergyman wheeling the Bath chair returned from his
length of the promenade, which Miss Steele pointed out.
"Though clergymen," she commented, "are always too
sober to be worth knowing. There's no gallantry about
them."

Louisa made her own first comment of the morning. "His
wife looks very ill."

"Well, they must have come here for her to have sea air."
As the Bath chair passed, Miss Steele waved gaily to the
gentleman, who gave her another grave nod. The
white-faced lady smiled at Louisa, who smiled uncertainly
back. "I wonder if we shall ever made any decent
acquaintance here," said Miss Steele, yawning. "It is
nothing but clergy, cripples and cut-you-offs. We must
notice the times of the public balls as we go back to the
house. I saw there was a concert tonight, but there is no
amusement in that – everyone has to sit mum and pretend
to listen a lot of scraping fiddles. I'd sooner play bezique –
Do you play that?"

"No, ma'am."

"Well, I am glad to hear it, the game bores me beyond
life. Come, I want to buy a parasol. With these feathers all
over my face it is no wonder not a soul looks at me."

By the perversity of nature, the acquisition of a pink
parasol heralded the end of the sunshine. Before evening,
the gathering clouds had brought rain. Miss Steele yawned
over her embroidery while Louisa sat contentedly reading
on the opposite side of the hearth. At every utterance of Miss
Steele's Louisa's eyes were lifted in polite half-attention but

no conversation took place. Miss Steele could not believe that anyone could be so absorbed by a book as the girl pretended to be. It was downright rudeness towards Miss Steele and she did not mean to put up with it. However, this interval gave her time to reflect upon the guineas in her purse, the shops of Brightsea and the comforts of this house. It would not do, to deprive herself of so much. Further, if Miss Steele left the girl to her books and went about the town on her own pleasures, who was to complain? Surely not the girl.

On the next day, matters were thus arranged. The rain had cleared, but the day was not bright enough for the parasol; nor, Miss Steele saw, were many people walking on the promenade. She devoted herself to the choice of gloves and hose and ribbons, but could not settle on a muslin for a gown; the choice was too wide. She returned to the house to find Miss Retford writing at the table, wearing her school apron as if that drab dress were worth protecting from her ink. Miss Steele told her so.

"And what are you writing anyway?"

"I am writing a letter to a friend."

"What friend?"

"My friend Rowena Parr who was at school with me."

"H'm," remarked Miss Steele looking over her shoulder, "I must say, they taught you a pretty hand at that school. I see you call this a pleasant house – myself, I should write it 'pleasent', but thank heaven it is no part of my work to correct your spelling. Why should you ask after Harold particularly?"

"Harold is Rowena's brother, and he recently broke his arm, in an accident while driving his curricle."

"He drives a curricle, does he, this beau of yours?"

"He is not ... a personal friend of mine, ma'am."

"So you say. Is he well looking?"

"I have never met him. I know only that Rowena is much concerned about him."

"About a brother? Well, I am sure he will soon heal.

These young rakes always drive too fast in their fancy carriages. My friend Mr Willis – he had a substantial ironmonger's business in Exeter but was quite the gentleman – once upset his carriage against a stone wall, and when I was told of it I was quite alarmed, it was a great joke because everyone twitted me as if he was a beau of mine, but indeed he was not. They say he was crippled for life, so I suppose he never married. Do you see these gloves I bought? Are they not the most striking shade of lilac?"

"Yes, ma'am," agreed Louisa glancing at them.

"Well, leave your writing now I am come in, and I shall show you what else I have bought." Miss Steele required an audience, however unresponsive.

"May I first write briefly to my grandfather? I ought to thank him for providing this pleasant house for me, and inquire after him."

"Oh, I am sure he does well enough, and he will not reply, if he is as ill as Mr Palmer says."

"Mrs Collier sometimes writes to me on his behalf."

"She is another of these clever women, is she? Make it a short letter, because I am ordering dinner soon. Afterwards I want to go to the Spring Pavilion to see if anything happens there. I asked where it is, and it is at the top of the town beyond that church. I expect I had better wear ..." Without finishing her sentence, because she had not decided what to wear, Miss Steele left the room to strive with the decision. When she returned, Miss Retford was putting away her writing-desk. Two letters lay on the table.

"Good, you have finished. We are to have roast mutton." Miss Steele had, so far, had no time for planning the household's catering; the servants seemed competent, and meals took second place to clothes. "What did you say to your grandfather?" she added, reaching for the letter.

"I am afraid I have sealed up my letter already."

"Oh, well, I am sure I have no curiosity to know. There is nothing you could have said except that you are happy here."

"Yes, I assured him of that." Louisa rose, unfastening her apron, and added: "I told him nothing about you, Miss Steele."

Miss Steele was at first annoyed; she would have expected herself to be a topic of primary interest in Miss Retford's present life, and a glowing description to be sent to Bristol. Her complacency was proof against a significance of the girl's expression as she spoke; Miss Steele expected Miss Retford to say nothing of great significance in any event. It was only after she had turned away to admire herself in the glass, still not entirely decided that the dressing of her hair was suitable to the Spring Pavilion, that she felt uneasy.

"I am sure I do not care whether you mention me to Mr Retford or not. Nor would he care for your opinion. It was fortunate for you both that I was at leisure to come here."

"It was, ma'am. But, should you find our tastes too dissimilar for your association with me to satisfy you, it is possible that another lady might eventually be found at leisure."

Miss Steele replied as she tweaked at a curl: "Oh, our tastes do not matter; you can read your books all day for all I care, and I am very well satisfied with Brightsea, or shall be as soon as I make some acquaintance here." But misgiving returned as she took in the latter part of Miss Retford's speech. The little puss might not be so tame as she seemed; *another* lady? Could she be so sneaky as to write to her grandfather complaining of her companion? One had to admit that Miss Steele was supposed to be here at Miss Retford's behest, humiliating as that was; and it was within Miss Retford's power to have Miss Steele dismissed. Miss Steele was slow to take a hint, especially so uncongenial a hint, but she was forced to admit that her position here might not be as secure as she had assumed. It was intolerable. Turning back from the glass she took the offensive:

"If I do not suit you, I am sure I am very sorry to hear it, but I do not see what I can lack as far as you are concerned.

One thing about me, all my friends will say – and I have never lacked for friends – I am always cheerful and ready for society and in amiable spirits. And, what is more, that is the kind of companion you are in need of. You ought at your age to be paying attention to your appearance and looking out for a husband, and that is where my duty lies, Miss, to see that you behave like a young lady of fashion and not like a tedious little bookworm. It is not for you to crticise *me*. Your grandfather desires me to set you out into the world and so I shall. I declare, these two days you have been downright uncivil, thinking of nothing beyond your own little affairs, and matters must be mended. Tomorrow I shall take you in hand and we shall have no more reading books."

Louisa had listened to this tirade tranquilly, standing by the table with her folded apron in her hands. As Miss Steele paused for breath, regretting already her own vehemence as she realised what she might have put at risk by it, she studied Louisa with private dismay, but could perceive the tranquillity and was as privately relieved to see it. Louisa said:

"I did not mean to be uncivil. I apologise."

"Well then, no harm is done."

"I agree," went on Louisa in a thoughtful tone,"that I do not care for the idea of balls or society, but that my grandfather wishes me to begin such a life, so I must obey him. However, there is a good deal of reading I still wish to do. Knowledge is more important to me than ball gowns. In that way, your tastes and mine may differ. It should be possible to compromise, I hope. If you do wish to remain in Brightsea, we can surely allow for one another's interests and devise a method of life that places us in accord."

Miss Steele took in, not ungratefully, the implications of this speech, the longest that Miss Retford had yet made to her. Taking in too the girl's composure, she said to herself: I suspect she is quite a clever little thing in her way, and not only from reading her books.

The suspicion was justified. Louisa had summed up Miss Steele as silly, affected and ignorant, but had calculated that these qualities might be turned to her own advantage. She felt no need of affection; she had been used to receiving so little that she might, in her present life, be happier with a companion who made no demands on her heart. She could observe that Miss Steele did not at all want to leave Brightsea; she could observe, in short, that with Miss Steele Louisa would be able to have her own way in everything of importance, while yielding on lesser issues. Louisa could handle Miss Steele; their association on this basis was acceptable to her.

Miss Steele also felt the better for this encounter. Miss Retford had apologised for her incivility, agreed to enter into society, and received her telling-off with due humility; Miss Steele should have no more trouble with her. So she could allow the girl to read her books for this evening and set off for the Spring Pavilion in gay anticipation.

The gaiety of the place did not fully rise to her hopes, but she was always ready to enjoy, and make the best of, fresh surroundings. The Pavilion was not spacious and the company for the most part elderly. Small groups conversed or walked, while a band played quietly; newspapers and gossip were exchanged. Miss Steele seated herself beside a doctor and his wife from Leicester, named Aylward, who told her that their son, also a doctor, was to visit them in Brightsea within a few days. "Perhaps we shall meet on the promenade, when the weather improves," Miss Steele suggested.

"I hope so," said Mrs Aylward, a sweet-faced woman in a gown whose trimming lacked lace, although its plainness was suitable perhaps to her age. "Oh," added Mrs Aylward as another lady crossed the room towards them, "here is my friend Mrs Mitchin. My dear –" to the lady, "we have made a fresh acquaintance –"

"How do you do," said Mrs Mitchin, staring at Miss Steele. "I have seen you yesterday in the town, have I not, walking with your daughter –"

"Indeed," cried Miss Steele with an indignant smile, "she is not my daughter. Why, she is all of sixteen years old and I – though I do not reveal my age – cannot suppose it appears sufficient to have a daughter of hers. Nor, I assure you, would I let a daughter of mine dress as she does. No, I am merely doing a kindness to her family, by having her to stay with me for the benefit of sea air."

Mrs Mitchin, whose seat Miss Steele had appropriated, made so little response to the information that Miss Steele soon removed herself in search of more agreeable company, reflecting that Mrs Mitchin's gown was even worse trimmed than Mrs Aylward's, and not heeding Mrs Mitchin's inquiry: "Who in the *world* ...?" as Miss Steele departed.

Miss Steele, reminded, determined to begin on the very next morning to improve Miss Retford's style of dress, since it reflected upon herself. Miss Retford, soon after breakfast, closed her book and made ready for the excursion; during which it rapidly became apparent to Miss Steele that the girl was quite silly and ignorant. She did not know tulle from voile, nor a ruche from a broderie.

Louisa, it was true, was wholly uninstructed in the sartorial arts; but her education bore fruit, in that she was ready to receive instruction. She was puzzled only by the discrepancies in it as offered by Miss Steele and the dressmaker.

"Let us have three widths of frilling," ordered Miss Steele. The dressmaker demurred, holding her pins suspended.

"Would that not be too elaborate, Madam, for such a young lady?"

"Lord, one can't be too elaborate for fashion, and she has plenty of money. Try a red satin for the sash; Louisa needs colour."

It was by accident, finding Miss Retford so much in this instance at her mercy, that Miss Steele fell into addressing

the girl by her first name. Louisa felt no objection. Dazzled
by the goods displayed to her and on her, she was slow to
form judgement; taste was as yet wholly unformed in her,
and she had never given thought to her appearance.
Regarding herself in the milliner's glass, in a bonnet of
velvet roses, she remarked: "I suppose my face is pale."

"Pale as putty," corroborated Miss Steele.

"But our sea air will soon restore mademoiselle's
colour," the milliner assured them. "Perhaps mademoiselle
has been unwell?"

Louisa had not; the doctor of her school had pointed out,
with justificiation, that she had spent too much time indoors
over her books, at risk to her lungs and posture. "Until such
a time," she suggested, "I should feel more at ease in a paler
colour."

"You have had enough of dull colours," Miss Steele told
her. "You must be cheered up."

"But perhaps this shade is too strong," the milliner said.
"And the velvet too heavy; more suitable for an older lady,
such as yourself, Madame."

Miss Steele had in fact been admiring the bonnet with
herself in mind, but after that insolence of the milliner's she
left the shop abruptly, Louisa following still puzzled. She
was thankful when she reached home, wearied out, to
resume her reading. After a while, however, she went to her
room to try on the fairly simple blue bonnet that had finally
been purchased, not in order to admire herself but to meet
herself anew in the guise of a young lady. Louisa was aware
that she must cease to be a schoolgirl, and was not
unwilling; only, a form of indolence, and strength of habit,
had allowed her to linger as she was. The glass now
reminded her that no great effort was required in growing
up; one had only to change one's bonnet. Upon which, one
became a young lady capable of her own decisions, free to
pursue her own thoughts, and dependent on no permission
of Miss Steele's for her actions. Louisa was quite without
personal vanity, which was as well, because she was not

pretty in her new bonnet; it was not beauty she aspired to, but independence.

It was independence of an inner kind, involving no rebellion. So it was in no spirit of defiance, but in calm determination, that on the next day she said to Miss Steele:

"There is a plan that I should like to carry out, could I find the means –"

"And what is that?" asked Miss Steele, twirling her pink parasol on her shoulder. The sun shone again, and the ladies were on the promenade. "I hope everyone is not noticing my parasol – I should hate to be stared at," she added, since no one had yet cast a glance at her. She and Louisa, each feeling she now had the measure of the other, were more at ease in conversation. Louisa went on to explain:

"While I was still at school, latterly I had begun to study Latin under one of our visiting tutors, and I would so much like to continue it."

"Good God, what is the use of Latin?" cried Miss Steele.

"It illuminates the structure of English grammar, and I much admire its economy and exactness of syntax," replied Louisa, taking the question not to be rhetorical.

"Oh, never mind that. It is just your bookish nonsense. You would do better to learn a modern tongue such as French. No one has learnt me such stuff as Latin and I have found no need for it."

"No?" said Louisa politely before proceeding: "I feel sure that in a neighbourhood such as this there may be some schoolmistress who could spare me perhaps one hour in the week –"

"A school *master* would more likely know Latin," pointed out Miss Steele, tilting her parasol as a pair of gentlemen passed; they kept their heads together in earnest discussion. "For that matter, several of these young men we see must know French or Italian."

"French and Italian I have studied already for some years. But you may be right; I think when we go to church

tomorrow I should inquire of the vicar, or curate.
Clergymen are necessarily Latinists, are they not?"

"Whatever they are, does not interest me," returned
Miss Steele. It did not interest her that Louisa was
interested in Latin. In her blue bonnet Louisa began to
appear more personable and amenable; at the same time,
Miss Steele recognised the resolution behind Louisa's
proposal. Very well then, conceded Miss Steele; fair
exchange: If she agrees to dress more fittingly, I shall let her
chase after her clergymen and Latin. Secretly Miss Steele
imagined that Louisa might not be easily prevented. This
was probably so; were it to come to a battle of wills, the will
of the mousy little frump could be the stronger. Nor did
Miss Steele, never bashful herself in approaching strangers,
wonder that Louisa was not timid in speaking to the
officiating clergyman after the service on the following
morning. The parish church, uphill of the crescent, was well
attended. Miss Steele saw the Aylwards there, and waited
in the hope of hearing that their son was come, but they left
by the further gate of the churchyard, among a crowd. She
was disappointed, nor did it gladden her that Louisa
rejoined her to say:

"Dr Mortimer was very kind. He hopes that one of his
curates may be able to give me lessons in Latin."

"Oh; a curate. I wish you joy of him." There was to be a
public ball in the next week, and Miss Steele already looked
forward to the description of it she would write to her sister.
She rose next morning impatient to go shopping for the
event, and was irritated that the manservant detained her
by saying:

"The Reverend Mr Dwyer has called, ma'am, about
Latin lessons for the young lady."

"Oh horrors. Well, send him up, quickly. Louisa!" she
called up the upper staircase, "here is your curate. Come
down and see to him, and do not be long about it."

Louisa appeared above, and at the same time from below
ascended the clergyman with the distinguished features,

whom she and Miss Steele had seen wheeling a Bath chair on the promenade. Recollecting him, Miss Steele let her severe expression soften. He was younger than she had remembered, but must be at least thirty – and, of course, he had a wife, but she looked very fragile and would probably not live long. She greeted him affably.

"I hope I am not calling at an inconvenient moment," he said.

"Not at all. You know Latin, do you, then?"

"To a moderate standard. You wish to be proficient in it?"

"Dear God, no. That is Louisa – Miss Retford. She is the one who cares about such nonsense. Louisa, here is Mr ... Dyer? Pray come into the drawing-room. You are in great luck, to have such a teacher offer himself."

Mr Dwyer, pausing only to assert his correct name, followed the ladies into the drawing-room and outlined the details of his offer. The difficulty arose only over the time of the lessons. Mr Dwyer said that the evenings would be most convenient for him, since: "My dear invalid retires early and I am likely to be free."

"Oh, but evenings, Louisa and me are not likely to be free. We want to go out to the balls and have some social life."

"I see. Then, may I suggest the earlier part of a morning? Are you," he asked Louisa, "an early riser?"

"Yes, sir, I am always up before seven."

"Well, that is more than I am," declared Miss Steele. "And," with a coy smile, "I am sure it would not be proper for you and Louisa to conduct your lessons unchaperoned."

"I did not propose to arrive as early as seven o'clock," replied Mr Dwyer seriously. It was settled for the present that when on two mornings of the week he had the duty of conducting the first service at the church, he would come thence to Stanley Crescent and give Louisa her lesson at nine. It was implied that his 'dear invalid' did not need his attendance until ten o'clock or so.

"So I am to have my hair dressed and be all ready by

nine, on two days of every week," complained Miss Steele when he had left.

"I do not suppose you need to do so on my account," said Louisa.

"No, nor on his either," admitted Miss Steele sighing. But she was spruce and ready for the first lesson next morning; and very dull it was. Not even a smile passed between master and student as they sat at the table. Listening, Miss Steele understood that Mr Dwyer was pleased, and surprised, by Louisa's aptness.

"... But you have a good grasp of the elements of the language already. I think we may even begin to construe some of Ovid ..."

Miss Steele yawned and dropped her scissors and wished to be back in bed; for all the notice taken of her, she might as well have been. Jealously she noticed that Louisa really must be told to sit up straight and not to frown as she pored over the pages; she was not trying in the least to make herself attactive. Clever she might be, but she could not hope any man would admire her the more for that. Mr Dwyer kept his eyes calmly on the pages and did not once raise them to Louisa's face.

However, there was the public ball to look forward to, in only two days' time; and this house, with a gentleman in it for whatever reason, became at once more animated.

4

On the next morning, of the day before the public ball, Miss Steele was threatened by another interruption in her preparations for that auspicious occasion. Louisa received a letter from Mrs Collier, on behalf of Mr Retford, requiring her to pay a visit in Brightsea.

"My grandfather has only now been told that Mrs Benson lives in the town," said Louisa, "and he wishes me to –"

"And who, may one ask, is Mrs Benson?"

"She is a nurse, and she nursed my grandmother in her last illness. I believe my grandfather found her very kind –"

"Well, if she was, that is no reason for you to go running about after her. She cannot be a genteel person and if she nursed your grandmother she must be old by now, if not dead. I suppose you do not want to renew your acquaintance with her."

"I do not remember her at all. My grandmother died before I was born. But I would like to visit her, Miss Steele, to please my grandfather."

"Oh, and I dare say she will be short of money, and will delay you for ever with her tales of woe, so we had better put her out of mind until after the ball. I have still to decide on the ribbons for my gown." She took the letter from Louisa's hand and added: "Besides, where is this Quay Street? Some mean part of the town that we would not want to be seen in. Nor do we know how to find it."

"We can ask the way," said Louisa in her reasonable tone which covered a mild obstinacy. Already Miss Steele was becoming wary of challenging it; assume authority as Miss Steele might, she had been for so long used to the domination of her own younger sister that she could yield, if petulantly, rather than invite conflict. So it came about that John their manservant was sent to discover the whereabouts of Quay Street while the ladies dressed for outdoors.

"All this charity-visiting will make us late for the shops, and the yellow ribbons will be sold out," lamented Miss Steele. "I marvel that your grandfather has not provided you with a carriage, which would save us our time. I swear he could afford to."

"He could, but I have no need of a carriage," said

Louisa. "I am to take exercise, and have no reason to travel far afield."

"Well, let us hope Quay Street is not far afield then."

"In so small a town, it could hardly be that."

"Oh, Lord, you will drive me mad with all your answering-back. Put on your better shawl, to show this Mrs What-was-her-name that we are not calling upon her except as a favour."

Quay Street was beyond the west end of the promenade, in a part of the town that pre-existed its development into a resort. As its name implied, the street belonged in the little fishing village that Brightsea had originally been. It was formed of small neat cottages, their cobbles swept and their gardens gay with flowers. The few inhabitants who were about stared in some surprise as the two ladies passed, to Miss Steele's gratification. It was Miss Steele's turn to stare, however, when she and Louisa were drawing near the cottage Mrs Collier's letter had specified. "That must be number eleven," Louisa was saying, just as the green-painted door of the cottage opened and a gentleman emerged, turning to bow to someone on its threshold, and putting on his hat. As he turned back to the street he almost collided into Miss Steele and Louisa, and his surprise was equal to Miss Steele's, so that he made a gesture towards raising his hat again, then bowed before walking on. He had wondered, Miss Steele could observe, what ladies of their quality were doing in such a part of the town, and she wondered as much at him. He was obviously not a resident. His bearing was good and he was finely dressed, probably about thirty years old, and with a face so striking that Miss Steele continued to stare at his retreating back.

Meanwhile the door of the cottage had closed again and Louisa unregardful of the departing stranger, was plying its knocker. A small woman in her mid-sixties, in neat white cap and apron, opened the door and admitted herself to be Mrs Benson. When she was told that Mr Retford's granddaughter confronted her, her rosy face broke into a beam of welcome.

"Why, what a morning I am having! Please to come in – Callers upon one another's heels – You must tell me how poor Mr Retford does – Dear, dear, it must be what – twenty years, since poor Mrs Retford passed away, yet he remembers me – Take that chair, my dear, and –" to Miss Steele, "if you, ma'am, would take this one – Wait, I must push off the cat – And you are Miss Retford? Then you are the child of poor Mr George, and not of poor Miss Alicia, because she, poor sweet lady, passed away before she married poor Captain Hyde, but he married later, and I was with his wife at her lying-in, poor lady, because the child was so frail ..." Her monologue ran on from one poor patient to another and it was with difficulty that Louisa managed to explain that her grandfather was not yet as 'poor' as they, and to convey his good wishes to Mrs Benson. Between them they conjectured that it was Mrs Collier who had lately sent the guinea that Mrs Benson received from Mr Retford on every birthday, though how Mrs Collier had maintained contact was barely explicable, so many had been Mrs Benson's changes of address. "... Although now I am retired from nursing, except when I am needed for emergency, as, only last week, a poor lady in lodgings at Prince's Place was taken ill with pleurisy –" And the poor lady had to be disposed of before Miss Steele could raise the question that had agitated her since their arrival at the cottage: the identity of the gentleman who had at that moment been leaving it. As Mrs Benson, full of energy and cheerfulness in spite of a lifetime spent in dealing with fatal afflictions, paused to run to a cupboard for cowslip wine to offer her guests, Miss Steele put her question without artifice.

"Oh yes, that was Mr Forgan, who is in lodgings in the town, and called on me, so kindly, though as well, he had some business to discuss, since it is only two years ago that I attended his poor wife." The adjective warned her hearers of the probable demise of Mr Forgan's wife, and they listened to the story of her illness before Miss Steele resumed:

"He does not live in Brightsea, then?"

"Oh, no, at that time they lived in Arundel, in a beautiful house. You could see the castle from its upper windows. I believe Mr Forgan gave up the house and went to London, but from what he says, he is not yet settled anywhere. Poor Mrs Forgan, and she had every advantage – so pretty, you know, and her family had money. But, they say, the good die young." She shook her head, more in acquiescence than in regret, and offered her visitors more wine. The cowslip wine's colour, however had reminded Miss Steele of yellow ribbons, and she was the more anxious to array herself for tomorrow's ball now that she hoped Mr Forgan, having been two years a widower, might attend it. Handsome, widower of a rich wife, and not a clergyman, he was the keenest spur to her optimism that Brightsea had yet provided. Rising, she said:

"Come, Louisa, we have business in the town."

Mrs Benson did not detain them, though urging Louisa to visit her again. "I hope," remarked Louisa as she and Miss Steele made their way back up Quay Street, "Mrs Benson will have no occasion to visit *me*. It seems, all her patients die."

"I did not listen to half her gloomy tales."

"She may still be a competent nurse. Do you suppose, persons with a cheerful outlook are more able to dwell on sad events?"

Miss Steele, whose own outlook was cheerful, dwelt neither on sad events nor idle speculation, but said: "Oh, hurry, Louisa, and do not chatter. I need those yellow ribbons more than anything in the world."

It was long since Miss Steele had had such an opportunity of dressing up in her best. In London, her sister often avoided having her invited to grand parties, and if Miss Steele were to go, criticised her dress and carped at her until Miss Steele felt quite confused and discouraged. With none

of Lucy's jealous nagging, and money to spend, Miss Steele
was in a frenzy of excitement as she prepared next evening
for the ball. Nothing went right. Her headdress toppled, her
new slippers would pinch her toes, her sash dragged –
"Molly!" she cried to the maid, "what are you about?
Come directly and help me –"

"I am seeing to Miss Retford's hair, ma'am," called back
the maid from the rear bedroom.

"Well, she can see to her own hair – The flounces of my
train are lying wrong, and – Oh la!" (an exclamation from
whose use Miss Steele's sister had been at pains to dissuade
her) "the ribbon is missing from my fan. Where can it have
gone – Good gracious, I cannot find my locket either, why
can you not be of some use –"

Louisa had been at some trouble to don the gown chosen
for her by Miss Steele, but having done so, she sat waiting
in the drawing-room perusing her Ovid while their hired
carriage waited outside. Louisa anticipated no great
pleasure in the evening and could not suppose, from the
tumult overhead, that Miss Steele either was in any state of
enjoyment. Louisa would attend the ball from a sense of
duty, and not to please Miss Steele; as she studied her Latin
because it interested her, and not to please Mr Dwyer. She
was not in the habit of pleasing others, but then, it would
not be exact to say that she pleased herself only. Her
pleasures, such as they were, were so inward and calm as to
seem negative. Neither she nor Miss Steele felt any interest
in the appearance Louisa presented when finally they
entered the ballroom.

Both ladies attracted the notice accorded to newcomers,
if in this instance it was mingled with some amazement or
amusement. Miss Steele parading the length of the room
and back before selecting a seat, gave the spectators a
display that she herself could well believe they had seldom
witnessed; tossing her head and twirling her fan, she kept
her gaze high, affecting not to care what impression she
made. In contrast, Louisa, eyes lowered, following, clearly

did not care; one or two puzzled glances returned to a girl so young and garishly clad whose thoughts appeared to be far away.

The room was not crowded, and Miss Steele placed herself and Louisa so they could command the whole view of it. "I am glad we arrived during an interval," said Miss Steele. "We shall have a chance to look about and see whether there is anyone worth dancing with. Do you see Mr Forgan here?"

"Who is Mr Forgan?"

"Louisa, for the Lord's sake sit up less straight and smile. Behave as if you were at a ball. He is the gentleman who had been visiting Mrs Benson yesterday."

"Yes; I had forgotten his name. I do not see him. Do you?"

"I am not going to stare about me as if I was seeking attention. Is there anyone else we have met?"

Louisa obediently stared about her. "I do not think so ... Yes, I remember a lady we passed on the promenade, with very dark eyes –"

"Never mind the ladies. Good, now the music is striking up." With her most charming smile, Miss Steele regarded the flounces of her skirt while fanning herself vigorously. A lady further along their seat confided:

"It is very hot in here, is it not?"

She was a portly middle-aged person whose pearls Miss Steele suspected to be false, but whose conversation offered at least a beginning. The lady, unfortunately, was garrulous, and bid fair to monopolise Miss Steele's company with descriptions of her widowed state, her large house in Aldgate and her brilliant son who was studying for the law. "I have told him to dance with Miss Zackerley, and so he did, but now he is run away again, for I see her dancing with Mr Betts, while Richard is not to be seen. Miss Zackerley, you know, is said to have twelve thousand pounds. Poor Richard is shy, that is his trouble. It is good for him to come to Brightsea – we come every year – and to forget his work for a while." By now the set was formed and the dance under way. Miss Steele hid a yawn behind her fan and asked:

"Are the balls here never more lively than this?"

"Do you not enjoy this? I find the room so well proportioned, in spite of its heat, and you will find the supper excellent. At the last ball, there was syllabub and a trifle made with clotted cream."

Miss Steele made no reply to that, having just noticed Mr Forgan dancing with a slender young lady in a white sprigged gown. At the end of the dance he passed without noticing Miss Steele, violently as she fanned herself. She had succeeded at any rate in catching the notice of the master of ceremonies, who as the music started again, bowed to her and Louisa and asked leave to present Mr Lee. Mr Lee, a smirking man with a face yellow as jaundice, inclined himself towards Louisa, but Miss Steele was already on her feet, and was at last dancing, bored as she was by Mr Lee's recital of his journeys in Morocco. When that set was over, again she passed close to Mr Forgan, and bowed to him; he ignored her. This time, Miss Steele knew that he had done so deliberately.

Seating herself again beside her portly friend, whose name had been given as Mrs Yarrow, she protested: "I was never at such a dull ball in my life. Louisa, we shall go home soon."

"Oh, no, you must wait for the supper!" Mrs Yarrow besought her. "And look – Here is Richard back. I wonder where he has been. Richard! He has heard me: he is coming. We shall get him to dance with your little friend. That will give her some pleasure. Tell me her name ...? Come, Richard, let me present you to Miss Retford. Why were you so long away? You must dance again. Make your request to Miss Retford."

If anyone could be more bored by this occasion than Miss Steele, it was Richard Yarrow, a pallid young man, as rotund as his mother, who wiped his brow with a kerchief and folded it tidily away before bowing and muttering:

"Miss Er ... may I request this dance?"

Louisa looked up quite surprised. "You must excuse me, sir," she said in her usual calm tone. "I do not know how to dance."

"Good gracious!" exclaimed Miss Steele, angrily. "Why not? How can you not know how to dance?"

"I have never been taught to," said Louisa by way of explanation.

"Then I do not think much of your marvellous education," cried Miss Steele snapping shut her fan. "You have wasted our evening, and Latin is all you are fit for."

5

In one particular, Miss Steele found Louisa as a companion unsatisfactory: she would not quarrel. Charged with slyness in concealing the fact that she could not dance, Louisa replied that she had been told she was to go to a ball but not that she would be expected to dance there; a piece of casuistry that provoked Miss Steele into further recriminations which left Louisa equally unmoved. It was punitively that Miss Steele ordered Louisa to take dancing lessons at once, so that she need not disgrace Miss Steele again on a public occasion. It was discovered that the dancing mistress of Mrs Bellwood's Academy for the Daughters of Gentlefolk would be prepared to give private lessons, and thither Louisa was to go on every morning until she was fit to stand up in society.

"Well then, after your Latin lessons on two of the

mornings, if you must have your own way about it," Miss Steele allowed on Louisa's protest. The protest was mild, and Louisa went off dressed for dancing with no further demur. Miss Steele felt chaperonage in this case unnecessary, and was happy to have extra time for her shopping; and Louisa was not unhappy in her instruction. Her natural movement was not ungainly, and she was quick to learn, in dancing as in bookwork. Her school had perhaps been remiss in allowing her her own way when she had chosen Italian lessons in place of the dancing class, because the exertion almost at once improved her posture and gait. Indeed, the sea air and less time for reading had, after only two weeks at Brightsea, been of benefit to her health. Her complexion was taking on some colour and her eyes, however pensive, shone brighter.

During the days that followed the ball Miss Steele was able to put its fiasco behind her and to appreciate that she was forming acquaintance in Brightsea; on the promenade she bowed to Dr and Mrs Aylward, Mr Lee of the Moroccan sunburn; of Mr Forgan she affected to despair, but Mrs Yarrow, usually alone and wondering where her shy son might be, offered to invite Miss Steele and Miss Retford to drink tea and make up a table for whist; and Mr Dwyer wheeling the Bath chair now smiled and bowed in a very friendly manner.

Louisa once observed: "Does it not seem to you, Miss Steele, that his wife is looking stronger? She is not so thin."

"Well, I dare say she will recover, then, though I do not know what has ailed her. Does he not speak of her to you?"

"Oh no. You must have heard that we speak of nothing but Latin."

"I am sure in your place I would have asked. Not that I suppose I am interested. I should like to know, all the same, his age, and why he is only a curate if he is so clever at Latin, and what does ail his wife. But you, Louisa, have too little curiosity about people."

If Louisa felt that Miss Steele had too much, she did not

say so. She said only, with a demureness that Miss Steele suspected to be her slyness: "I imagine Mr Dwyer's wife has not been attended by Mrs Benson, if her health is on the mend. Shall we," she added, "visit Mrs Benson again soon? I should like to see her."

"Oh, you may go on your own. I have no time for tales of death. But, if you want to know about Mr Dwyer's wife, your idea is not a bad one, for nurses are the most amazing gossips in the world."

Louisa, again, did not trouble to defend her motives in wishing to visit Mrs Benson, nor to deny that she herself sought gossip. It was true that, while she took her lessons from Mr Dwyer, she gave all her attention to the work; which Miss Steele had come to suppose, to the effect that she did not chaperone the lessons now, being tired of completing her toilette by nine of a morning. Her curiosity about Mr Dwyer's affairs was not sufficient to force her to that effort, fine-looking as she still considered him. It was of no use to curl one's hair for someone who, after one civil bow of greeting, never looked in one's direction again.

The topic of Mr Dwyer, however, presently arose in another connection that caused Miss Steele consternation. After a week of fine weather, during which Louisa practised her dancing and called on Mrs Benson, and Miss Steele anticipated the arrival of the Aylwards' doctor son, Miss Steele received a letter from Mr Retford's solicitors, who dealt normally with his financial affairs as Mrs Collier with his domestic.

The letter stated without urgency that the solicitors would find it sufficient were Miss Steele to render the household's accounts to them once in every month, although she was no doubt keeping her expenditure noted on a weekly basis.

Miss Steele was thrown into a fright. She had been keeping nothing of the sort, and there was every doubt that she could render an account to the solicitors. As usual, when things went amiss it was the fault of everyone but

Miss Steele. She threw the servants into a consternation as great as her own, if with less justification, for Molly, Rebecca and John were neither dishonest nor extravagant, nor was it for them to pay tradesmen's bills or assess the establishment's resources; and, under so careless a mistress, who disbursed what was required as soon as asked, it was small wonder that financial affairs were as haphazard below stairs as above.

"La, how careless the lot of you have been," scolded Miss Steele with papers crumpled before her over the table. "Here is the grocer wanting seventeen shilling for apricots – I ordered none at such a price –"

"No, ma'am," indicated Molly. "That is in addition to the bill for the previous week, which was not paid."

"And why was it not? You should have brought it to me, and as for the apricots, I remember none – I dare say you ate them yourselves in the kitchen, and have cheated me out of Lord knows what else – What does this scrawl mean, on the washing bill?"

John was himself baffled for a moment before he recollected: "That was last week, that I had to borrow a shilling out of the washing money to pay Peter who could not wait."

"And who pray is Peter?"

"He comes of a Monday, ma'am, to clean the front windows and the railings. He does so for the owner of the house, he told us."

"Well, I will have no Peters spunging on me. Whoever owns the house should pay for his railings to be washed. How am I to know what is going on, when I am told nothing? And how am I to make up the accounts, when you have let all fall into such confusion?" She ran her hands through the papers before her, tossing them as if haymaking. To owe a shilling to the washerwoman was a scale of debt to which Miss Steele was fairly well accustomed; the rest of this predicament was beyond her. The servants stood mute under her reproaches, unable to help.

The person probably most competent to help was Louisa, but Miss Steele was not going to be so undignified as to appeal to her, for all Louisa's cleverness. And at this juncture Louisa, who had been standing by as mute as the servants, laid a paper on the table saying:

"Here is another bill, Miss Steele, which was brought this morning addressed to me."

Miss Steele snatched it up. "To tuition in ballroom dancing, seven hours at one half-guinea ...' Lord, Louisa," she cried, "how like you to make matters more difficult, when I am so much pressed already!"

"I am sorry. I thought that, while you are dealing with the bills, you would wish to include them all up to date."

Miss Steele, far from dealing with the bills, was far from grateful for Louisa's contribution. "You thought only of aggravating me. You and your dancing are nothing but a nuisance. If you had been learnt dancing at school as you should have been, there need have been no bill – And I am sure," she recollected, "next minute you will throw at me another bill for all your lessons in Latin. You have been saving it to spite me like all these others."

Louisa looked surprised. "No, ma'am, Mr Dwyer has never said anything to me about payment for my lessons with him."

"And I expect you were too busy burying yourself in your books to ask him about it. You will tell me he wants twice as much as the dancing mistress. It is your morning for Latin tomorrow, a'nt it? You must have it out with him."

"Indeed, I hardly like to mention it to him."

"Well, you had better, or if you are too cowardly I will put it to him myself. I am driven quite out of my mind. Genteel persons do not usually have to deal with money." With a scornful air she rose and swept all the bills into a heap, adding: "My head aches beyond endurance. I am going to walk to the Spring Pavilion. You may come if you want."

"Miss Steele, I could pay the dancing mistress from my own money –"

"Do as you like. I have heard enough of these sordid money matters for today," declared Miss Steele, waving her hand in dismissal. On the next day, however, she woke with some unusual weight upon her spirits. She lay for a while pitying herself. How had it come about that she, so full of liveliness, with a nature made for gaiety, who had done no harm to anyone, should be expected to cope with obstacles such as household bills? One needed, as well as wanted, a husband. At the very notion some energy revived; she remembered that Mr Dwyer was to come this morning – indeed, from her clock, he should be already here – and that she must ask him about the payment for his lessons. Dressing in haste, her hair covered, she went to the drawing-room.

Here Louisa and Mr Dwyer were at the table, whence the heap of bills had been removed. Mr Dwyer was reading aloud in his steady voice:

" '*Quod apes cum stirpe necatas …*' The participle, you see, agrees with the plural noun –"

"Mr Dwyer," interrupted Miss Steele, "I am sure Louisa has not given you the message I charged her with."

"Good morning to you," said Mr Dwyer rising. "What message was that?"

"Well, she tells me you have not asked any payment for your lessons, and while I am making up the accounts for the solicitors, I shall need to know, so you might be good enough to write me out a bill."

Mr Dwyer appeared slightly amused. "My dear Miss Steele, there is no question of payment. It is a pleasure to me to teach, and adds variety to my occupations. Indeed, I find that I am learning some Latin myself in reading with Miss Retford and I enjoy our sessions."

"All very fine, but nobody gives nothing for nothing in this world, and your curacy cannot be worth much. Besides, Louisa is rich."

"I am happy for her that it should be so. My own income, however, would not be significantly increased by a tutor's fees paid twice in the week."

Distrusting him – for who could not want money? – Miss Steele insisted: "Do not act so much the gentleman, Mr Dwyer. I know you have more than one curate in the parish, and that you must have much outlay in the treatment and medicines for your wife."

He seemed, at that, surprised; then he said: "I believe we have not discussed my circumstances before, so you are under some misapprehension. I should perhaps explain that Dorothea is not my wife, but my sister. We were left orphans at an early age, and have always been closely attached to one another. When I was ordained I took up a family living in Staffordshire and Dorothea came to keep house for me. She was stricken with her illness about a year ago, and as soon as the doctors pronounced her out of danger but in need of a long and careful convalescence, I had no course but to devote myself to her, and so I confided my duties to a friend and we both removed to Brightsea. To convince Dorothea that I was making no sacrifice for her sake, I undertook to assist Dr Mortimer – one of whose curates, as it happened, had just quitted him for the mission fields – without remuneration, for as long as I am required to remain here."

Miss Steele and Louisa listened to this recital attentively. It was Louisa who spoke first as it ended:

"And is Mrs – Miss ... Dwyer improving? I had imagined so?"

"Yes, by God's mercy, she has regained much of her health even in the last few weeks."

Miss Steele's reflections on Mr Dwyer's story pursued a different course. She thought: A family living, which means a family of some respectability; and money, if he can afford to pay for his sister's treatment and work besides for nothing. And no wife, after all. He must be thirty years old (in fact Miss Steele could not allow any eligible gentleman to be under the age of thirty) and I always thought him gentlemanly-looking. And that little puss Louisa has had him to herself unchaperoned these many hours; not that she would know how to make use of the opportunity.

In a much more amiable tone Miss Steele said: "Then, if you can afford not to be paid, that is a relief, for the work these bills are giving me is terrible. Well, excuse me not having my hair dressed yet, but I dare say we shall see you later, on the promenade." It was by now time for Mr Dwyer to leave, so he quitted the room ahead of her. Miss Steele lingered to say:

"So, Louisa, your poor curate is not so poor after all. Be sure you treat him with respect, and do not go making yourself familiar to him."

Louisa did not answer that admonition, but said: "This morning, I gathered up your papers from the table, and I have tied them into packets according to their kind. I found that some of your own bills, from the draper's for instance, had become mixed into the household bills. I hope I have set all in order."

To be sure you would, said Miss Steele to herself. If my small bills were to go along with the domestic ones, what would be the harm? It is no concern of yours, Miss.

Miss Steele had at one point contemplated submitting a bill for Latin lessons to the solicitors and pocketing the proceeds, but she decided that Louisa would no doubt find out, and give her away. She was not very affably disposed towards Louisa this morning.

6

The later part of that day was rainy, so after Louisa returned from her dancing lesson the ladies made no further excursions. Louisa at the table wrote, she said when asked, to Mrs Collier. "And I do not doubt you tell her some false tales about me," was one of Miss Steele's remarks that Louisa did not answer. In emulation, it occurred to Miss Steele to write, as she had not yet, to her sister. She penned a long description of the magnificence of the house, the splendours of the shops and the social delights of Brightsea; the public ball came in for special praise. '... I had many partners of course such as a gentleman who had travelled in Africa and my gown was not torn tho the train was so long ...' and, wearied by this literary labour, she had little to add about Louisa. Her grievances against Louisa would possibly not add to the impression she wished to make on Lucy; so she ended: 'My freind Miss Retford is very clever and a gentleman we met who is from a rich family in Staffordshire comes to visit us and read Latin with her and that is why he says he comes but he is much older than her and I beg you not to tease me, becuase there are many more here. I wish you were here, you would enjoy it so much. Yr affectionate sister, Nancy.'

"There," she said, sealing her letter with great firmness, "I will not tell you what I have told about *you*."

Louisa, whose own letter mainly concerned Mrs Benson, had no curiosity to know. The letters were taken to the post next day, when the capricious spring had returned again in fuller warmth and the promenade was thronged with parasols. Miss Steele and Louisa had not been a half-hour in the parade before they saw the Bath chair coming towards them. Today, Mr Dwyer halted, and introduced Miss Dwyer to them.

"I am so pleased to make your acquaintance at last," said Miss Dwyer, smiling. "And I do hope you can forgive me, that I have not spoken to you sooner. I really was not equal to conversation, but I have been much interested in all Martin told me of you."

"I hope it was all of it complimentary," said Miss Steele, laughing.

"It is you," said Miss Dwyer to Louisa, "who are

progressing so well in Latin? I wonder why you should wish to learn it?"

"So that I can read, in the original language, some of the great orators, and poets," said Louisa with animation. "I want to read Virgil, and of the exploits of Aeneas. Then I would like to read Greek, to study Homer."

"I fancy," observed Mr Dwyer from his post at the handles of the chair, "that Miss Retford will achieve any ambition she aims at. She is a diligent scholar, and we hope to begin the Aeneid soon."

"I already know how to scan a hexameter," said Louisa with an eagerness that Miss Steele took for self-praise.

"Now, Louisa," Miss Steele said, "stop showing yourself off with long words. You must excuse her, ma'am, she is not much used to society."

"I hope I shall have more of her society myself soon, when I am free of this chair and able to walk. I feel strong enough already to attempt it, but my brother is very strict with me."

"Oh, I am sure he knows what is best for you. There will be time enough for society when you have your looks back, and are able to come to the balls."

Miss Dwyer offered her thin hand to each of them, and her chair was wheeled on. Louisa said: "How much better she seems. I am so glad. I wonder if she reads Latin and Greek herself?"

"If she does, it has done her health no good, nor got her a husband," remarked Miss Steele. "I detest these clever women. They affect such a superior manner, there is no rational talking with them." All at once, her attention was caught by another figure walking towards them: it was Mr Forgan, walking briskly and alone. Scarcely had Miss Steele begun to twirl her parasol when he stopped and bowed.

"May I presume to present myself? I have the honour, I believe, of addressing Miss ... Steele, and Miss Retford?"

His manner was formal, but easy, and his smile made his face no less attractive. Miss Steele's astonishment allowed her only to blurt:

"How do you know that?"

"I am indebted to Mrs Benson, whom I had the impertinence to ask for your names, when I called upon her yesterday. We did meet in passing outside her house, previously, as you may remember."

"Of c – No, I do not. That is, it may be. I think I saw you at the ball, after that, but you did not remember me then."

"For that I must apologise, though I admit I did not observe you on that occasion. In future, I shall hope that you remember me, and permit me to make what amends I can for my ignorance."

Miss Steele was recovering her composure. She said in a jocund tone: "Aye, gentlemen are always ready to promise amends, and to plead their ignorance. At the next ball, we shall see how your memory serves."

"My memory, as you observe, is today in excellent working order. If you are proposing to come to the concert this evening at the Spring Pavilion, you may put it to the test."

"There is a concert, is there? Certainly we intend to be there."

"Then," he said, looking from Miss Steele to Louisa, "I look forward to pursuing our acquaintance." With more apologies for his effrontery in introducing himself, he bowed again and walked on.

"I wonder," said Louisa, "why he should suddenly wish to know us?"

"Lord, Louisa, you quibble into everything. He explained, that he had asked Mrs Benson about us. Besides, it was not you he was speaking to, so you have no need to wonder anything."

"You wish to go the concert? I believed you did not care for music."

"Well, I do. If you do not care for music you need not come."

"I am fond of music," said Louisa in her peaceable tone.

"One would not have imagined so, since you have never

yet wanted to go to a concert here. Now, you change your tune."

Louisa had deferred to Miss Steele so far in the matter of concerts, but did not argue the point. She said only:

"Was it not this evening that we had engaged to drink tea with Mrs Yarrow?"

"La, was it? It cannot be helped. We shall make what excuse we can. You can write a note in that pretty hand of yours and John shall take it to her. Who would play whist with that fat woman and her unmannerly son when there is a concert to go to? Now, stop making difficulties, and let us turn back, because I shall need fresh lace for my green gown if we are to go into company, and Rebecca will need time to sew it on. How vexing that I have posted my letter to Lucy before this, but I can write again, because I shall have more to tell her soon."

Miss Steele's social horizon was expanding in a rapid and most gratifying manner. For the concert in the evening she clad herself in the freshly elaborated green gown, and out-shone in her own opinion all the other ladies present, who were dressed as soberly as if for a mere dinner-party. She soon perceived Mr Forgan, who arrived among a small group, and was in a fidget until he had caught her eye and bowed. As the music was about to begin, Mr Dwyer entered the room also, with an elderly nondescript lady on his arm. Miss Steele must wait for his greeting until the intermission, since everyone was intent on listening and no eyes, except hers, wandered. She controlled her impatience, and amused herself by studying the dress of the audience and swinging her locket to and fro on its chain. She need fear no rivalry from Mr Dwyer's companion, who must be eighty years old at least; and she was reasonably sure that the lady beside Mr Forgan was the wife of the gentleman on her other side. The fourth member of that group, a short man with a snub nose, she after a brief survey disregarded; he was not well-looking at all. Each time there was applause, Miss Steele shook out her frills ready to rise, but, each time, the orchestra struck up again and the tiresome singer resumed her caterwauling.

The singer, unknown to Miss Steele, was to the older members of her audience famous on the London operatic stage, from which she had lately retired. She was giving a series of concerts about the country, in the nature of a farewell, and the musical younger listeners were anxious to be able to tell their children that they had once heard Alessandra Rossi sing. Or so Miss Steele understood from the conversation, when at last the intermission came, and Mr Forgan had introduced her and Louisa to his friends. From the despatch with which Miss Steele approached when the audience was circulating, he could have done nothing else, but he did so willingly. He was staying, it seemed, with Mr and Mrs King, while the short snub-nosed man was presented as Signor Jacomo.

"Her voice," said Mr King speaking of the singer, "is past its fullness, but her artistry is still superb. Do you not agree?" he turned to Miss Steele, who replied:

"I do not know about artistry, but I have seen none of her paintings. I thought, she made a terrible screeching."

Mr King gave her a startled look, while Signor Jacomo threw back his head and laughed. Miss Steele deduced that she had said something very witty, and in modestly fanning herself missed the reproving nudge that Mr Forgan gave the small man before he asked Louisa:

"And what did you think of Signora Rossi, Miss Retford? Have you heard her sing before?"

"No, I have not," Louisa said, and after a moment's thought added: "It seemed to me that the orchestra was too heavy. I would rather have heard her with a pianoforte only."

"I quite agree with you. Her voice may have lost power, but it has gained in delicacy, and that is what the accompaniment obscured."

"Her next group of songs is to be in Italian," said Mr King. "The language should allow her more expression."

"Lord, is she to sing in a foreign language? Then she will be even less worth hearing," remarked Miss Steele. Signor Jacomo, now quite serious, said to Mr King:

"In the Albinoni in particular she will find her full flexibility."

Miss Steele, tired of this solemn conversation, looked aside and saw Mr Dwyer carrying a glass of wine towards his elderly lady. Miss Steele prodded him with her fan, to the hazard of the wine, and cried:

"How d'ye do, Mr Dwyer; are you another of those who do not remember a face at an evening party? Is that your mother you have there? I thought you said you and your sister was orphans."

Mr Dwyer, pausing to explain that he was escorting Dr Mortimer's mother, had perforce to be introduced to Miss Steele's group. Mr and Mrs King, he had met in church; Mr Forgan, Miss Steele fancied, gave Mr Dwyer a very measuring look, which was returned. It was to her highly diverting, to watch the two rivals for her favour confront one another. Laughing, she pursued:

"And what are you doing with that wine? Where is it from?"

"I am taking it to Mrs Mortimer, since she does not wish to move from her chair. I have brought it from the supper-room."

"Is there a supper? Then why," inquired Miss Steele at large, "are we all dallying here?"

Mrs King took up, speaking to her husband: "Yes Frederick, do let us have a little supper. The intermission must be half over." She took her husband's arm; Mr Forgan, whom Louisa still detained in solemn discussion of music, observed what was intended, and gave his arm to Louisa; Miss Steele and Signor Jacomo were left, with little enthusiasm, to face each other. The small man said:

"May I take you to supper, then, Miss Steele?"

"Oh, very well, Mr Yakko." (Or whatever his name might be.) They followed the others into the side room of the Pavilion, where a slight but tasteful collation was laid out. Mr Forgan was compelled to sit by Louisa, but Miss Steele thrust past Signor Jacomo so that she could face Mr Forgan. "I dare say Louisa has been telling you," she called to him, "that she has learnt Italian, so will be able to understand the songs that are to come next."

"Do you know Italian?" Mr Forgan asked Louisa.

"Oh yes," answered Miss Steele for her. "There is no end to her being educated. Mr Dwyer, who you have just met, teaches her Latin, and she is learning to dance. She must learn fast, for no one can be at such a place as Brightsea and not be able to appear at its balls."

"Do you enjoy dancing?" Mr Forgan still addressed Louisa.

"I do," Louisa said, "but I should hesitate as yet to stand up at a public ball and do so."

"Then, when next we have a ball, you must allow me to stand up with you and give you encouragement. Your hesitation will give way."

"Oh, Mr Forgan," cried Miss Steele, "Louisa would not care to be so singled out. She is very young, and besides is not fond of society. She cares about nothing beyond her books. You mean to be kind, but it is me you should ask whether she is to dance with you, because she is in my charge, her grandfather has set me over her to look out for her, and I cannot have her taking up with gentlemen strange to me."

Mr Forgan looked with half-inquiry at Louisa, who sat with lowered eyes and her normal calm lack of expression. After reflecting to himself for a moment he said: "I understand," and, taking a fruit dish from the table, recommended the figs to Miss Steele, offering to pick out for her the sweetest and ripest. Gratified by this attention, she was further flattered that he said as they rose from the table: "I hope there will soon be another ball, for, whatever Miss Retford's reluctance, I must not let myself remain unknown to her guardian angel."

In spite of the screeching Italian arias that followed the intermission, Miss Steele returned home from the concert in high good humour. "You see, Louisa," she said as she pulled off her tight slippers, "the concert was not so bad after all. There was the supper, and we met so many friends. Poor Mr Dwyer, having to look after that horrid old hag Dr Mortimer's mother, after looking after his ghost of a sister all day, besides taking church services; I hardly wonder he finds Latin a relief, but that is hardly cheerful either. He should learn to dance as well, and then if he came to the balls I should soon cheer him up, but as for you dancing with Mr Forgan, you need not be afraid I shall let you. He meant it kindly, and I told him so, but you need not dance at all until you feel quite ready to."

"If we go to another ball," said Louisa who had been pursuing her own thoughts, "I think I would like a new gown –"

"Mercy girl, you had a new gown and have worn it only the once!"

"Yes. But I observed, when we were at the ball, that most of the girls of my age were more simply dressed than I was. Many of them wore white. I think I should like a white gown, of muslin, perhaps with spots or sprigs of a light colour."

"Oh, very well, if you want to make yourself look dull and simple," conceded Miss Steele, not entirely displeased. "We shall go to the draper's tomorrow and then visit the dressmaker." The prospect of any shopping always stirred her. "In fact I believe there is another ball announced for next Friday, so you will have to hurry with your dress. I shall wear my pink again, I expect, but I must have a new sash, which will mean new lacing too on the bodice, I dare say, because the stuff I had matches with the sash. Lord, how busy we are, and what a deal there is to be done. See, here is a note left on the table –" She tore it open. "Oh; Mrs Yarrow was sorry to hear of my indisposition and hopes we can drink tea with her on Thursday next instead. I dare say we had better. My green will do for that, if I have Rebecca take off the lace, which I do not think suits after all. I declare, we live a delightful life here; I wish it could go on for ever."

Louisa did not echo the wish. Nevertheless, when after the process with the dressmaker she regarded herself in the glass, in a white muslin gown with glossy spots, her hair as glossy, her cheeks softly coloured, she thought: I believe I could dance as well as many of those other girls: indeed, I now look very much like them; no one would notice me among them. The notion gave her a strange new satisfaction.

Miss Steele remarked to the dressmaker: "She would not stand out in a crowd, but she looks tidy enough. I suppose it takes someone of my style and bearing to carry off more striking colours."

7

The effect of Miss Steele's letter on her sister was just as she had hoped. Lucy was astonished, incredulous, and bitterly envious that Nancy should have secured to herself a friend so rich and clever and generous as this Miss Retford, and moreover secured an invitation to pass the whole summer in a fashionable seaside resort whereat, from Miss Steele's account, the society and entertainment was the most diverting in the world.

As Lucy's mind dwelt on the affair, however, the sentiment that came to dominate those of her first reaction was incredulity. Sisterly charity saw it as beyond belief that anyone who was clever should choose to associate closely with Nancy, or that Nancy should be making so many conquests among the beaux of such a place as Brightsea; and as for the new gowns and bonnets so copiously mentioned, Lucy could not suppose Miss Retford lavish enough to subscribe to such outlay. "I only hope," said Lucy to herself, "Nancy is not running up bills in order to come pleading to me as she so often has, to be rescued from the penury in which she truly deserves to live. And I hope she remembers by the way that she owes me I cannot reckon how much, for the debts to me that she has never paid, let alone for her keep in my house for these many years."

Lucy had found her sister a confidante and sometimes a support, without finding her discreet, reliable or necessarily truthful. Nancy had been occasionally useful but more often, especially of late, a nuisance. When Nancy took herself off to visit the Palmers in February Lucy had been thankful to put Nancy out of her mind. This unexpected development from the visit rendered Lucy puzzled and suspicious. It occurred to her that the Palmers were probably by now in London, and that she might seek some explanation from them. Dignity would not allow her to call on them with direct inquiry, but she would surely meet them sooner or later.

Within a few days, she encountered them, at an evening party given by Mrs Palmer's sister Lady Middleton. She contrived to draw Mrs Palmer aside and, after due inquiries about the children, added:

"My sister made some new acquaintance while she was visiting you?"

"Did she? Yes, of course, she was with us for some weeks, but we had no other company. Unless you are speaking of the Blakes, but it was not while Nancy was with us that they came to dinner, I now remember."

"I was referring to her friend Miss Retford, with whom she is now staying. She is well known to you, I suppose?"

"Oh yes, Nancy is gone to Eastbourne, is she not? Or Worthing. She has taken my sable tippet with her, but it is no matter, I never wear it. On occasion I find it useful, but she might send me some money so that I can buy a new one, if I need it."

"I wonder that Nancy could afford what that would cost."

"Oh, yes, she will be able to afford it, I dare say, for fur does not cost a great deal, although it comes expensive. Now I think of it, I had a letter from Nancy, and she seems in good health. I am glad it was arranged that she should go to Miss Retford, are you not? You will miss her, at home, but you are so much occupied, I expect you have little time to think of her."

"Miss Retford," Lucy persisted, "is well known to you?"

"Oh dear, yes, not that I have met her, but Mr Palmer is very close to her family. She has no family, I believe, excepting her grandfather. So she has been at school, though I think she has now left it."

"She is only young, then?"

"Oh, a child merely. But now she must be a young lady."

"And Nancy tells me she is wealthy?"

"Yes, indeed, her grandfather's house in Bristol is splendid, and it will all come I suppose to Miss Retford. It seems the house in – is it not Brightsea? – is splendid too. It was all so lucky for Nancy, and it was Mr Palmer who had the idea, you know; he is so ingenious, and takes such pains to help others, when he thinks of them."

"What was Mr Palmer's idea?" asked Lucy with a sharpness that made Mrs Palmer recollect her own discretion.

"Why, he spoke to old Mr Retford, but I of course was not present, so I do not know what was said. You must not ask me what Nancy asked me not to say, though I am sure I forget now what it was. Please excuse me, dear Mrs Ferrars – Mr Holland is waiting to speak to me –" And she fled, leaving Lucy to seek out Mr Palmer forthwith. Mr Palmer offered at once the information that Lucy had wasted so much time in failing to obtain from his wife; no one had warned him to withhold it, and he was pleased with his success in removing Miss Steele from his household. "I wonder," he remarked, "you had not thought of something of the kind earlier. I do not suppose she will do well in the position," he ended with his usual civility, "but she would do well in nothing else either."

Lucy went home from the party in thoughtful mood. Anger at Nancy's duplicity began to subside as Lucy sought a way of turning it to her own advantage.

Ten years of marriage had refined Lucy Ferrars's manners without performing the same service for her mind. She had needed to keep her wits about her even after persuading Robert Ferrars into a runaway wedding, since his family had required a great deal more persuasion before he was forgiven for it. Lucy had been as charming and obsequious as the situation demanded, and finally established herself in graces as good as could be expected of old Mrs Ferrars, whose autocratic governance of her family no one disputed. Her two sons were very unlike in character and circumstances, one being a country clergyman, and the other a fashionable man about London. Mrs Ferrars's disapprobation was visited upon each in turn according to her whim, and it was Lucy who suffered most under her caprices; the clerical household was undisturbed by them, being at a distance safe from any but rare visits and prudent in financial matters; while Robert, reckless in defying his mother as in squandering his money, left it to Lucy to repair his damage, not least to her own nerves. Continual exercise of flattery, parsimony, recriminations and guile were telling upon her; lately she had fancied her face thinner and a frowning line graven into her forehead; her beauty was forsaking her. It was untimely to hear of Nancy dancing about Brightsea in new gowns.

Before she retired that night, Lucy re-read her sister's letter, the frown sharp on her brow. "No, my dear Nancy," she said aloud, "it is not about your beau from Staffordshire that I shall tease you." As soon as her domestic affairs were set in order next morning she wrote a reply to the letter:

"My dear Nancy: I am very happy to know that you have a gay time in Brightsea and that you have found so excellent a friend as Miss Retford. As she is so well disposed, and as the house is so spacious, would it not be a good scheme for me to bring the children to visit you? I am sure now the weather is warmer a little sea bathing would do me good, and you know Augusta has never lost the cough that troubled her last winter, and sea air would quite restore her. I shall be pleased to see you and need be no infliction upon Miss Retford."

Lucy read this over, reflecting that it would be a fine tease for her sister to be taken up on her story of being a personal friend of Miss Retford. Nancy could hardly seize her pen to confess that she was in Brightsea only as a paid companion. Of course, when Lucy arrived, all must be admitted, but Lucy did not imagine Nancy quick enough to think so far ahead. However, lest Nancy try to prevent her, Lucy added to her letter:

'The children eat so little, I am sure you will be at no extra expense, and if you have money for new bonnets, it may be you can contribute a little for our keep, for certainly I have been at some expense for your keep for so long, and I am at present in some difficulties with R.'s owings, so it would be hard to take you back here, and so it suits me well that you are established away until the autumn if not longer.' Which was a strong hint that if Miss Steele were to offer no hospitality to her sister, she might expect none in return.

It suited Lucy well, also, to make a visit at present: Robert himself was away, horse-racing with friends, having taken with him all the money he could lay hands on; which did not include a sum that his wife kept hidden for these emergencies, and which would be sufficient to convey herself and her children to Brightsea, where she proposed to spend nothing but to rest until her looks and nerves improved. She knew herself able to procure an invitation from anyone by her own means, even from any Miss Retford, but she preferred in this instance to tease Nancy.

The letter, reaching Brightsea, threw Miss Steele into an alarm that would have gratified its writer. "Gracious heaven," she cried in a voice that was almost a shriek, "here is my sister wants to come to Brightsea! And to bring her children. What am I to do?"

Louisa, unstudied in family relationships, assumed the shriek to have been of delight, and applied her sympathy in practical fashion to Miss Steele's question. "Do you mean that your sister wishes you to seek out lodgings for her? I expect the town is full, as Mrs Yarrow was telling us. But, could your sister and her children not stay in this house with us? There are bedrooms empty."

That Lucy fully intended to stay in this house, Miss Steele did not reveal. She herself was so little disposed to welcome Lucy here that she could summon no gratitude to Louisa, nor appreciate that the invitation had been given unsolicited, sparing Miss Steele the embarrassment of angling for it. Embarrassment arose only because now Lucy would find out that Miss Steele had descended to paid employment. "I wish now," Miss Steele protested to herself, "that I had told Lucy the truth at the outset, because then she would not have thrust herself in like this; servants do not receive their relations as visitors." She could not guess that Lucy, professing ignorance, had out-thought her on that point as on others. In reply to Louisa Miss Steele said:

"Then I dare say they must come. Lucy," as she looked again at the letter, "pretends she is short of money, but so she always does, and I do not know why, when all that family is so rich. I do not know who is to pay you for having her."

"But indeed," said Louisa surprised, and more embarrassed than Miss Steele, "there can be no question of any payment."

"Well then, let us hope there is no trouble about all that."

Opportunely, the letter had arrived on the morning of the second public ball, whereat Louisa was to try out her dancing and to wear her white gown, while Miss Steele in her new sash and her equally new feathered head-dress was to make her usual striking appearance. This prospect enabled her to put Lucy's letter out of mind. Mr Forgan had surely promised to dance with her, while who knew who else might be there, now that the season was advancing into summer and more visitors arriving. Miss Steele was still disappointed of the Aylwards' doctor son, who had been, his mother said when inquired of on the promenade, delayed. The Aylwards were still accompanied by that disagreeable Mrs Mitchin, whom further inquiries from Miss Steele discovered to be a widow. Under closer scrutiny, Mrs Mitchin seemed younger than Miss Steele had fancied; to Louisa Miss Steele confided: "It is that ill-natured expression of hers that makes her look so old. You can wager, she hangs about with the Aylwards in hopes of catching the son for herself. Well, we have friends enough now, and need not deprive her."

In the ballroom on this Friday, several faces were indeed known to Miss Steele, although the crowds made movement difficult. She and Louisa were forced to seat themselves beside Mrs Yarrow, who complained with reason of the heat of the room and, with no reason acceptable to Miss Steele, of the absence of her son Richard. At the whist table this young man had shown his manners to be no more gracious than in the ballroom. Mrs Yarrow said: "I do not know where he can be ..." and added in a whisper to Miss Steele; "How very sweet your little friend looks tonight."

"Louisa? She chose that gown for herself. I have nothing new on, except for this sash, and these pink plumes to match it." As Mrs Yarrow spoke the necessary compliments Miss Steele did not listen, intent on looking about for Mr Forgan. When she saw him she was at first discouraged to discern him among a large party. He was dancing at present with Mrs King, but when he drew near to Miss Steele and caught her expectant eyes he at once bowed and smiled. At the end of the dance he approached and asked Miss Steele to stand up with him, adding that he hoped she and Miss Retford would honour his party by joining it.

"Come, Louisa," cried Miss Steele, rising, "you can sit by Mrs King or someone while I dance." At the same moment, however, Mrs Yarrow at her other side exclaimed:

"Here is Richard! Where have you been? I am sure Miss Retford is waiting for you to renew your invitation to her."

Richard Yarrow mopped his forehead, while Louisa murmured a disclaimer, but Miss Steele commanded her: "Go along, Louisa, and dance with Mr Yarrow. You can join us after that." And without a backward glance she laid her hand on Mr Forgan's arm to be led into the set.

He danced, as she already knew, very well, and agreed with her praise of her gown and feathers. Miss Steele enjoyed herself mightily. It was only as they stood in a pause that she noticed his attention drawn away from her. In an abrupt tone he asked:

"Who is that puppy?"

Following his gaze she saw that he was watching Richard Yarrow and Louisa, who after some hesitation had joined the set lower. Miss Steele answered in surprise: "He and his mother are very respectable acquaintances I have made. Louisa and me have drunk tea with them. He is too young for me, of course, but will do well enough for Louisa."

"His mother I do not doubt is respectable. But as the young man stood close to me I fancied I caught spirits on his breath." He added with deference: "Since you are, I believe, responsible for Miss Retford's well-being, you may permit me to put you on your guard? Ladies such as yourself may not have my own experience of judging character."

"I have experience enough to know a drunken man when I see one," returned Miss Steele, tartly. "As for Louisa's well-being, you can be sure my judgement of character would not let any undesirables near her."

Mr Forgan regarded her as if weighing that, before he said: "I am glad to believe you. Later, with your permission, I shall ask Miss Retford to dance. If you remember, I told her that I wished to know how proficient her lessons had rendered her."

"Did you? She might not remember. But, yes, ask her if you want to. I do not know who else will."

To himself, Mr Forgan said: "She may find Luigi a helpful partner, if she lacks confidence."

"And pray who is Loo-jee?" asked Miss Steele.

"– I meant my friend Signor Jacomo, whom I presented to you on the night of the concert at the Spring Pavilion."

"Is *he* here? Upon my word, Mr Forgan, you have no right to complain of my choice of friends when you have such peculiar ones of your own. He is a foreigner, is he not? Am I supposed to think such people fit to associate with Louisa?"

At his most persuasive, Mr Forgan managed to apologise for Signor Jacomo and for his own unintended criticism of Miss Steele's choice of friends, while at the same time explaining that Luigi Jacomo was nevertheless a gentleman eminent to musical circles, Italian by birth, but often resident in England, which was demonstrated by his perfection in the English language; he spoke French as perfectly, having in the course of his career as a singing teacher spent much time in Paris. To all of which Miss Steele replied only: "Oh; he is a teacher, then, is he?" before turning away her attention as a method of drawing Mr Forgan's back to herself.

At the end of the dance, Mr Forgan led Miss Steele towards the end of the room where his own friends were gathered, without observing that Richard Yarrow, bowing languidly to Louisa, had walked off abandoning her in the middle of the floor. Louisa, searching among the dispersing couples, could perceive neither Miss Steele nor Mrs Yarrow, and was uncertain of her direction; it was the young lady from Mr Forgan's group who cried: "Why, that poor girl is lost!" and hurried to bring Louisa to join the party. "Sit here beside me," she begged Louisa, "and tell me about yourself. I am Isabella King, and I am here with my aunt and uncle, which may surprise you, since Mrs King seems too young to be an aunt, but, you see, Mr King's father was twice married ..." And she rattled through her family's history before pursuing her inquiry into Louisa's. "Tell me, is it your aunt you are with? I have seen you these many times about the town but it was not till now that I dared approach you; you seem," she confided, artlessly, "quite different this evening. A white gown suits you so much better. Tell me, who is the fat young man you danced with? He did not seem to have a word to say for himself; which," she admitted, laughing, "is not a failing of mine."

Louisa, laughing too, disclaimed relationship with Miss Steele, to some apparent reassurance of Miss King, who rattled on, reminding Louisa of Rowena Parr, at school; Miss King was three years older than Louisa, but seemed to have more in common with her than anyone else she had met since coming to Brightsea. At the end of the evening, when she and Miss Steele were home, Louisa was still animated; asked whether she had enjoyed the ball, she said:

"Oh, yes, ma'am; Miss King was so kind. She said I might go walking with her. She knows of a path that leads over the cliffs."

"But what of the dancing? I suppose it is all right for you to walk with Miss King, if you do not fall over any cliffs. What did Mr Forgan say when you danced with him? You both looked grave."

"He said that my musical sense was good, and my step would become lighter with practice."

"Indeed, that was not very gallant of him. You must learn to be more cheerful if you want to attract your partners. Then he made you dance with that little foreigner, who should have given you more instruction on your musical sense, as he is a teacher of it."

"Signor Jacomo?" After reflection Louisa said: "I felt, a little, as if he were privately laughing at me."

"I cannot see why," said Miss Steele, not caring either, since Louisa evidently did not, and in any case it was her own story of the evening that Miss Steele was impatient to unfold. She saw it as successful, and according to her nature, gained impetus from any success towards an even brighter future; Mr Forgan had danced twice with her, had mentioned that he might stay on in Brightsea for longer than he had intended, and had spoken of sailing boats and sea trips; meanwhile Louisa, between her Latin and dancing lessons, and her walks with Miss King, should be no encumbrance; and when Miss Steele recollected the advent of Lucy, she now saw no reason to dread that, for indeed she longed to show Lucy her new wardrobe and surroundings; a married lady without her husband should not go much into company; Lucy with her sea bathing and her children to occupy her should be no encumbrance either, and might, when one thought of it, be the very person to deal with those tiresome household books and bills. Miss Steele decided to write to her sister promptly, bidding her welcome.

8

Welcome was not what Lucy Ferrars had expected in reply to her self-invitation, and she was ungenerous enough to wonder: "Can Nancy be up to some trick?" She proceeded with the preparations for her visit undeterred, as no trick of

Nancy's had ever outwitted her own. She had little curiosity about the society of Brightsea, or that of Nancy's immediate circle, but nevertheless was a little surprised to find Miss Retford so unlike her half-expectation. Nancy had described Miss Retford as 'clever', but in comparison with Nancy, so would anyone appear; whereas anyone under Nancy's governance must be as foolish and affected as she. Lucy had submitted to no governance of Nancy's when she herself was of Miss Retford's age, knowing herself the stronger character. She could not associate strength of character with a girl so unassuming as Miss Retford, since her own had been displayed in defiance and wilfulness; she wondered that Miss Retford could tolerate Nancy as she did, without perceiving the quiet wilfulness that gained Louisa her own way in most matters yet avoided conflict. Conceding that Miss Retford was clever in her way, studying Latin and so on, Lucy considered her simple in the ways of the world, and yet could not dismiss her as negligible; her intuition suspected that unobtrusiveness. She was envious too of someone so rich, well educated, and young; beauty Miss Retford might not possess, but those attributes Lucy knew herself lacking in, and her civility towards Miss Retford as her hostess covered a grudging gratitude.

Whatever the qualities of Miss Retford, Nancy was quite as Lucy had expected to find her: full of herself and her dress and her beaux, heedless of her extravagance, of Louisa, and of the duties of housekeeper. It was marvellous to Lucy, knowing nothing of Miss Worthington and her negative contribution to the appointment, that Nancy should have been thought eligible to take charge of such a household, and in the glow of affection that often illuminated, however briefly, a reunion between the sisters, Lucy responded to Nancy's plaints by agreeing to oversee the household's accounts: "... When I am rested." It would be to no one's advantage were Miss Steele to be shown up as incompetent.

Meanwhile, rest was what Lucy desired and intended.

The day following her arrival was fine; she disposed of her children by telling her nursemaid to take them away and keep them quiet, while Miss Steele disposed of Louisa by sending her to call on Miss King; then the two sisters walked on the promenade, where a surprise awaited Lucy. She had, habitually, discounted Nancy's tales of her beaux and fine friends, and had not expected that within the length of the promenade Nancy should be greeted by Dr and Mrs Aylward, Mr Dwyer and his sister, and finally by Mr Forgan, who was walking with Miss King; nor that Mr Forgan's manner towards Miss Steele would be so amiable. As a beau, he was well above Nancy's usual standard.

"Miss Retford is gone to call on me?" cried Miss King when she had inquired after her new friend. "Then I must return to the house at once, and hope she has waited for me. Mr Forgan, will you please to tell my aunt where I am, when you meet her?"

"It might be better, were I to accompany you home," said Mr Forgan. "I have undertaken to escort you, and Mrs King would not like you to go alone about the town."

"I am sure you need not fear," protested Miss Steele. "So is Louisa gone alone from Stanley Crescent to Buckingham Place, which is about the town, if not so far; and here are *two* ladies also in need of an escort," she added, twirling her parasol. And, upon Miss King's denying that she needed escort, Mr Forgan yielded, and remained walking with the two sisters for some while, until Mrs King had completed her errands and joined them. Further introductions resulted in an invitation to an evening party at the Kings', extended to Miss Steele, Mrs Ferrars and Miss Retford. Miss Steele announced at once that her sister was not in health for society, but Mrs Ferrars instantly contradicted that, and the engagement was set.

"It was Mr Forgan who made Mrs King ask us," Miss Steele reminded her sister when they had turned for home. "Did you notice? Now Lucy, you are not to start teasing me, nor start Louisa either."

"Do not worry; I shall not. He is several years younger than you," Lucy mentioned in a dismissive tone.

"He is a *widower*," stated Miss Steele with dignity. Lucy did not see how that pertained to the question, but nevertheless she had been struck by Mr Forgan's attentiveness to Nancy and was, unflattering as it may have been to her sister, at a loss to explain it. Mr Forgan was, by her impression of him, a man of intelligence as well as of taste.

At that same moment, Isabella King was asking Louisa: "What is your impression of Mr Forgan?"

The two girls were following a path that led from the gardens of the Spring Pavilion to the cliff-top, Louisa, a little breathless from the climb, paused as usual to consider a question exactly before replying:

"I find him very pleasant." She neither knew nor wondered why Miss King should ask, but, as Miss King too paused, as if expecting the topic to be pursued, she offered:

"Have you know him long?"

"Since he lost his wife he has spent a deal of time with my uncle and aunt," said Miss King. "And I, too, am often there, because my father is abroad. He is ... very amiable in company, and conceals his own feelings bravely."

"Your father?"

"No, no. Mr Forgan." The exercise, or the fresh breeze at this height, had raised a colour in Miss King's cheeks. "Shall we walk on? We shall not have time today to complete the circuit, but I can show you the view from the cliff point." She resumed as they walked: "I admired his bearing at the time of his loss, although I dared say nothing to indicate how deeply I sympathised with him."

"Were you acquainted with his wife?"

"A little ... He bore his bereavement with great dignity, and his spirits have improved, as I had hoped and trusted they would. He is ready, I think, to make new friends and attachments now. After two years, is that not to be expected?"

"Yes," decided Louisa. She halted again to look down. On their eminence they had passed beyond the old village of Brightsea and now stood above open sea, broken into by ribs of rock that formed little coves in the cliff. Sensing that Miss King, however, was not finished with the subject of Mr Forgan, she brought her mind back to him and added: "He is certainly ready to be agreeable in present society, from what I have seen of him. He was very kind when he danced with me at the ball. And," now she thought of it, "he appears to be making a friend of Miss Steele."

"Oh; do you think so?" answered Miss King in a distant and dejected tone. "Of course, one readily forms acquaintance at such a place as Brightsea, and, as you say, he is always prepared to be agreeable ... When he let me leave him this morning, it was because he had barely been introduced to Mrs Ferrars, and must have felt – It was he," she interrupted herself, "who, after the ball, praised me for taking notice of you, and recommended me to seek your friendship, which in any case I would have done, I assure you," she ended more warmly.

"I am very grateful to you."

"Nonsense, the gratitude should be mine. What is Miss Steele's age, do you know?"

"No, nor would I dare to ask her."

Louisa had said this with her customary seriousness, and was surprised that Miss King laughed so merrily, linking her arm in Louisa's and meeting her eyes sidelong as if they shared a joke. Infected, Louisa smiled too, and they proceeded to the cliff point in great amity. When they turned back they agreed that they must share another walk soon, and each, returning home, was pleased to be told that she was to meet her friend again at the Kings' evening party.

Lucy Ferrars was not much pleased to be going to the party. She had accepted the invitation because Nancy refused it for her, and so was disposed to blame Nancy for committing her to it, and as she had brought no party-dress from London, to demand the loan of Nancy's yellow tulle; Nancy objected that she had not yet worn the gown herself, to which Lucy retorted that Nancy already possessed more gowns than she could pay for; Nancy, after referring to Lucy's comparative wealth, demanded her ambers to wear with the yellow, adding that no doubt Lucy had left those too in London? The ambers, Lucy insisted, had been a present to her, and she had no high opinion of people who asked for their presents back.

This altercation took place between Miss Steele in her bedroom doorway and Mrs Ferrars in the doorway of her room above, and so was audible throughout most of the house. Louisa, already bewildered by several encounters of this nature between the sisters, was the more disconcerted on this occasion because her Latin lesson was in progress, and Mr Dwyer must either raise his own voice above the voices outside, or cease his exposition of the Predicative Dative. As she looked up, she observed that a third person was in the room: Lucy's son George Ferrars. He had been trapped in here by the arrival of Mr Dwyer, and had meant to creep out unnoticed, but as he reached the door the quarrel outside arrested him. He stood with his back to the room and his hand on the knob of the door, rigid, as if afraid either to go out or turn back.

Louisa had seen little as yet of George or his smaller sister Augusta, and had heard less. She did not know that their mother had warned them sternly against obtruding upon Miss Retford's notice. Lucy was fond of her children, and proud of George's quickness and Augusta's prettiness, but she was determined that no child of hers should be spoilt. She had suffered sorely in earlier years, when visiting friends whose good opinion she must strive for, from being therefore obliged to indulge their already over-indulged infants; besides, her nerves would not stand any crying or stubbornness; she had checked her children so severely that sometimes they turned pale at the very sound of her voice. George was now nearly eight years old, an upstanding and intelligent boy, but his own nerves were not equal to his immediate predicament. As Louisa called him, in an uncertain voice: "George?" he turned as uncertainly back towards her with tears on his pale cheeks. It was Mr Dwyer who took up:

"What is the matter, my boy?"

"Oh, sir, I am so very sorry," said George in a whisper. "I was on the sofa reading, and I know I am not allowed in this room, but when you came in I thought of hiding, but then I knew I should not, and I was hoping you would not notice me –"

"Why should you hide from us?" asked Mr Dwyer in his gentle tone. He held out his hand, and George came reluctantly to the table.

"We are to stay in the back parlour with Jenny," he said. "But then I heard my mother and my Aunt Nancy ... They would be cross with me –"

"No one will be cross with you. Do not be afraid. Miss Retford, shall we ask Master George to stay with us while we finish our lesson? You see, George, some of the books have pictures in; you can look at those while we read."

Louisa smiled at George, who, thus encouraged, came to look at her reading book. "Oh, but, sir," he said, "I know some of the words too. We learn Latin now at my school. This –" pointing "– is a picture of a Roman soldier, and beneath it, '*in bello contra*' means 'in the war against' – but I do not know the next word –"

"It means 'the Gauls'," Mr Dwyer told him; and he added to Louisa: "It appears you have a rival." He drew up another chair and George, his chin on his hands, listened with appreciation as the Predicative Dative's exposition was continued. By the end of the hour he was pink-faced and gleeful. "When I am back at school I shall surprise them by all I have learnt – that is, if I might, please, listen to you again?"

"Certainly you may," Louisa told him.

"You see, I should be at school now, but my mother

wanted to bring us to the sea. I shall miss the last four weeks of term. I am glad to be at the sea, but sorry to miss my lessons."

Louisa had already recognised a fellow enthusiast, and she had pitied the boy on seeing that he was afraid of his mother; in truth, Mrs Ferrars frightened Louisa a little at times.

Not that this much troubled her; indeed, Louisa had troubled herself very little in her life about other people. Her apparent hard-heartedness came about, however, through a natural and compelled solitariness, and not through any self-interest; it took no more than this morning's prick of compassion for a little boy to awaken her latent affections. She was fully aware for the first time of the importance of these; she began to look about her, wondering; she observed with a new gratitude how very kind Mr Dwyer was; her smile as she bade him farewell had a new and timid gentleness, and she asked with real concern after Miss Dwyer.

In the same new consciousness she approached the evening party at the Kings'. It now seemed to her that her friend Miss King was in some disturbance of spirits; observant, Louisa presently wondered: "Can she love Mr Forgan?" If so, Louisa was anxious on Miss King's account, because Mr Forgan during the evening paid her no attention. Card tables, and round games, did not wholly occupy the company; there was much movement and conversation, and Mr Forgan directed his mainly to Miss Steele and Mrs Ferrars. Miss King came after a while to sit beside Louisa, and said with suppressed agitation:

"Miss Steele is very gay tonight. I am sure her cheerful manners must recommend her to – anyone. Mrs Ferrars, I think you told me, is not a widow?"

"No. Mr Ferrars is visiting other friends."

"She, too, is very attractive," said Miss King with some air of relief. "I see Signor Jacomo is back from London; he has been away these two days. I wish I did not distrust him.

I always feel he is laughing at us all."

"I have felt the same," agreed Louisa. "He stays here with you?"

"Yes, he is a close friend of Mr Forgan. I cannot but wonder at that. He gave singing lessons, you know, to Mrs Forgan – Mr Forgan's late wife – before her illness, so they have known each other a long while. He gave singing lessons to Mrs King, but she does not think well of her own ability."

Mrs King's opinion was evidently not shared by her husband, who in a pause after supper called to her: "Come, my dear, let us have some music. Let us hear one of your songs, and Signor Jacomo will accompany you."

"Oh, but I am out of practice, and dare not sing while Luigi is here," Mrs King cried; but her guests must in politeness support her husband, and Signor Jacomo had already gone to open the pianoforte and put on his eyeglasses. He was laughing at nothing now; as he laid out the pages of music his face was almost grim. He consulted with Mrs King over what song she might attempt, and meanwhile Mr Forgan crossed the room and seated himself by Louisa, on the opposite side from Miss King. "I shall like to have your judgement of the music," he told Louisa.

"But I know nothing of singing, sir."

"I might be so discourteous as to deny that, after the discussion we had on Signora Rossi. You at any rate listen to music, which is rare."

"But many people listen."

"They pretend to. But you take it seriously."

"I believe," Louisa said, "that Signor Jacomo does."

"Yes, Luigi is very much in earnest about music. You yourself, if I am allowed to say so, take the whole of life seriously; your nature is sincere and earnest."

"I do not know what my nature is," said Louisa drawing a little back, lest Miss King should feel herself excluded.

"No, your lack of vanity is most engaging."

Louisa need not answer that, as the consultation by the

pianoforte was over, and Mrs King was permitted to begin
'Hark, hark, the lark.' Her voice was sweet, and had been
well trained, but that could not conceal its slightness.
Signor Jacomo did not entirely disapprove of her
performance, to her evident consolation, and another
consultation over the music books began, while Mr Forgan
remarked to Louisa:

"In spite of Shakespeare's excellent diction, I think I
prefer that song in its German translation. I feel that music,
like poetry, has its true source in the language of its
creator."

"Then poetry cannot be translated?" said Louisa, her
interest caught. "I know that many people think not." They
entered on a discussion of language, and Mr Forgan's own
grave interest drew her out into speaking of her enjoyment
of Latin, her regret that it had not been taught at her
school, and of George Ferrars whose school had taught him
so much of it already.

"He must be a little prig," said Mr Forgan smiling.

"Oh, no. He is a very lively boy, when he is allowed to
speak." Recollecting, Louisa drew back again and added:
"Miss King and I have invited him to come with us when
we walk on the cliffs, and he is full of excitement at the
idea."

Mr Forgan looked grave again. "It is a kind idea of yours,
but I wonder whether young ladies should take the
responsibility for leading an excited little boy along the
cliff-tops. There are dangerous spots. I should be happy if
you would allow me to walk with you, and easier in my own
mind."

Louisa was glad for Miss King that this offer had arisen,
and could not help liking Mr Forgan herself, for his
thoughtfulness and his equally thoughtful conversation.
After another song from Mrs King, the party reassembled
for more games, and Mr Forgan was summoned away.
Louisa was surprised when Miss King said:

"You had a great success with Mr Forgan."

"Did I? But we were merely talking of languages."

Miss King regarded Louisa closely, then laughed and admitted: "I suppose you were. Well, so we are to have him with us on our cliff walk. I hope," with a sigh, "little George will not mind his coming."

Louisa could deduce from that over-casual sigh that Miss King did not at all mind Mr Forgan's coming. She determined to keep George close by herself, and to release Mr Forgan to Miss King.

On the next morning, when she mentioned at breakfast the scheme of the cliff walk, Miss Steele at once cried:

"Mr Forgan is to come? I do not see why we need not all walk on the cliffs. I feel the need of fresher air."

Mrs Ferrars said: "Nancy, do not be pushing yourself in." Miss Steele was offended, but Louisa not ungrateful for the intervention.

9

Lucy Ferrars, as is not uncommon, assumed the motives of others to be similar to her own. Before she had been long at Brightsea she had assessed the motives of Mr Forgan: he was on the lookout for a rich wife. Lucy's sharp eye had noticed that his clothes, although of fine cut, were not new; that he lodged with friends instead of taking a house of his own; that he mixed much in society and had a charm of manner that could adapt itself to any company. She decided, further, that Mr Forgan had selected Louisa Retford to fulfil his requirements, and that he was pursuing her with care. He had seen that in order to approach Louisa he must first secure the favour of Miss Steele to bypass her guard and jealousy, and that in approaching Louisa herself he must be as solemn as was consonant with charm. Lucy wished him all success, and found the spectacle mildly diverting. She said nothing to Nancy, who should at her age be able to look out for herself; Lucy could not help it if her sister chose to make a spectacle of herself, parading in her finery and revelling in flattery; malice in Lucy anticipated Nancy's disillusionment. As for Louisa Retford, she would find in Mr Forgan a good enough husband; she was a dull and innocent creature, but with a stubbornness that would allow him not all of his own way. Probably she would read her books and he would lead his own life unregarded; almost any husband would do for her.

As for this walk over the cliffs, Nancy should realise that to thrust herself into the party would do her no good. The others would walk too fast for her and she would grow hot and dishevelled, and it would be plain that she was literally chasing Mr Forgan. Some sense of delicacy must be preserved. Nancy, who could never accept advice, was angry, but Lucy firm. When Mr Forgan and Miss King called at Stanley Crescent for the other pair, Lucy was as firm with her son.

"Now, George, you are not to chatter and be a nuisance. You hear?"

"Yes, ma'am," said George, pale after Jenny's scrubbing and his mother's admonition. He took Louisa's hand as they set off.

If Mr Forgan were ready to adapt his manner to any company, this morning he chose to adapt it to George's. As they reached the cliff path he drew George near the edge, holding him by the arms, and pointed out the sea birds flying below, and the little sandy bays between the rocks. "Do you see, when the tide is low a boat can be brought in, by a skilled boatman, and there must be caves beneath us, where smuggled goods can be hidden."

"What are smuggled goods?" asked George round-eyed.

"Well, it might be, casks of spirits, or rare fabrics, or pirates' treasure."

"Treasure?" cried George.

"Then, when the tides are high, the excise officers cannot reach the caves: nor at low tide have they time to search them all. Come, we must rejoin the ladies."

Louisa was much pleased by this attention shown to George, and the more disposed to feel herself at ease with Mr Forgan. She endeavoured as they moved on to retain George and to let Miss King walk with Mr Forgan, but George, wild with freedom, ran too fast for her, chasing the gulls and throwing his cap at rabbits. "He will not go near the edge, alone?" she appealed to Mr Forgan.

"I shall see that he does not. Come, let us all sit and rest now. The turf is dry and we can admire the view."

They were at the point of the cliffs, whence they could see all of Brightsea laid out behind them, from the fishing village in the foreground to the glittering windows of the Spring Pavilion above the trees and white villas of the town. "There are boats in the harbour," Louisa pointed out. "And I believe I can see Quay Street, where Mrs Benson lives."

"Ah, yes; Mrs Benson," said Mr Forgan. "You visit her often?"

"Twice, only. I have not seen her recently."

Mr Forgan, a little troubled, said: "I could wish you need not."

"Why is that?"

"The low-lying area of the town is not healthy."

"But Mrs Benson's cottage is neat and clean –"

"Yes, of course. She is a worthy woman in her way, and I am not at liberty to disclose anything I know to her disadvantage. It would be asking a great favour, to expect you to discontinue the acquaintance."

Louisa remembered his saying that he had 'business' with Mrs Benson. "But you are no friend of hers?" she suggested.

"Rather, there are friends of Mrs Benson's whom I would not consider fit for your association."

George who had been listening cried: "Is this Mrs Benson a smuggler, then, sir?"

The others could not help laughing, but Louisa sensed that Mr Forgan met her eyes with significance before he said: "The boats you see in the harbour must have come in on the morning tide from fishing, and will be unloading their catch. The lower town at present must be distinctly malodorous."

"But we are not going there," said Miss King. "Shall we not turn inland, and return through the woods?"

"What would Miss Retford choose?"

"It is all strange and delightful to me," said Louisa. "I am happy to follow any way Miss King prefers."

"Let it be the woods, then," agreed Mr Forgan rising; Miss King quickly put out a hand, to be helped to her feet, while Louisa was still occupied in re-tying her bonnet ribbon.

Louisa, after that morning, liked Mr Forgan a good deal better, but was not the more persuaded to relinquish her acquaintance with Mrs Benson. Nor was she the more resolved to renew it; Mr Forgan's implied warning had stirred no curiosity in her, and she did not imagine that Mrs Benson was necessarily pleased by Louisa's visits. When she found the time, Louisa would perhaps go to see Mrs Benson again, but time was seldom to spare. With her Latin, her dancing, her walks with Miss King, her games with George and Augusta in the back parlour, and her evening engagements, Louisa filled her letters to Mrs Collier with busy happiness; and if Mrs Collier did not quite understand how the house in Stanley Crescent came to be filled with Georges and Jennys and Mr Forgans, she at any rate understood that Louisa was leading a life more suitable than that of her bookish childhood, and let well alone, as she supposed.

Mr Forgan did seem to be more often about the house

lately, but as far as Louisa supposed, he came to call on Miss Steele; she had no idea of what Lucy fancied to be his pursuit of herself, and was sorry only for Miss King. With Miss King, she had an increasing sympathy, though she dared not speak to her of Mr Forgan unless Miss King began on the subject; which she not infrequently did.

"I was surprised that Mr Forgan did not join us today on our walk into the woods."

"I thought, when he came, that he meant to suggest it. But Miss Steele asked him to go with her to the sea shore, to inquire about the bathing."

"Oh: she intends to have sea bathing, does she?"

"It was for Mrs Ferrars, I believe. The weather is now warm enough –"

"For Mrs Ferrars? Yet Miss Steele went ... He is very obliging."

"If he calls tomorrow morning, I shall try to be the first to ask him to come with us and George to the cliffs again."

"Oh, if you are to ask him, I have no doubt he will come."

Miss King's friendliness was not, at present, as warm as it had been. Louisa ascribed this only to her disappointments over Mr Forgan.

Louisa's increasing sympathy with Miss King had its echo in herself. It happened that, one day as she was returning with George from the shops where he had wanted to buy a potato gun, she noticed a pair of figures on the other side of the street: a gentleman and a lady walking arm in arm. Before she had recognised them, the sight of the gentleman gave her a shock of pleasure. She had had barely time to admit this when George cried:

"There is Mr Dwyer! I must show him my gun." He ran off across the road, and Louisa following already attributed her pleasure to the recognition of Miss Dwyer, delivered from her Bath chair. She was still frail, but had been able to walk with her brother's support as far as the bookshop. "I must go home now," she told George, "but perhaps you will come and visit me soon, with Miss Retford, and show me how your gun works."

"Yes, ma'am, I will. I shall not kill anything, you know."

Mr Dwyer said to Louisa: "Do you know where our house is? May we arrange a time? Or should Master George first ask his mother's leave?"

"Perhaps he should," agreed Louisa. A hint of complicity in Mr Dwyer's smile gave her strange satisfaction. After that, she began to try even harder over her Latin, yet in spite of it, made more mistakes. It seemed more difficult to keep her attention on her book. When George, who still joined their lessons, said something that made Mr Dwyer laugh, the light of the whole room seemed to brighten. Louisa took a slightly fearful pleasure in these symptoms without asking herself what they were indicative of.

She and George were permitted to visit the Dwyers' house, where Miss Dwyer sat in a long chair in the garden admiring George's prowess with the potato gun. Mrs Ferrars had said only: "Well, if Louisa wants to take up with these friends of hers, I suppose it takes George out of our way." Mrs Ferrars, Louisa inferred, was not enjoying her sea bathing; she said that the air had done nothing for her complexion, nor Nancy's tantrums anything for her nerves, and she might soon return to London, since her husband had not been heard from and she must discover what mischief he was up to. The prospect of losing George gave some alarm to Louisa, and so did another notion that followed upon it, and that she forced herself with unusual diffidence to voice to Mr Dwyer:

"I suppose, that as Miss Dwyer is so much recovered, you will soon be going home to Staffordshire?"

"We have not planned to," he answered. "In truth, we expect to stay in Brightsea until October."

Later in that morning Miss Steele, in good humour, called across the passage: "Louisa, is that you singing? I have never heard you sing before, and you have quite a pretty little voice. We shall have to have Mr Yakko give you lessons."

The little snub-nosed Italian polyglot was still intermittently of their circle, but meanwhile the society of Brightsea changed as visitors came and went: more came than went, and Lucy Ferrars complained that one could not move in the shopping streets, while Miss Steele pushed her way through the throngs as inquisitive of every new face as she was of every item in the shop windows. Lucy was, on the whole, becoming bored. She treated herself to a new gown in order to go to the next ball here, but saw little object in that, since she could not engage in her sister's amusement of amassing beaux; incidentally to which, she was beginning to wonder what had become of Robert; she had had no news of him since his disappearance to Doncaster, or Chester, or wherever he had omitted to mention; it was possible that Lucy's reciprocal disappearance might not have the desired effect. Robert would not care where his wife was, but his family might regard her prolonged absence with a disapproval Lucy preferred not to court. Incidentally to the topic of courting, it was at the ball that Lucy became impatient that Mr Forgan had not yet declared himself to Louisa Retford. It was while the two of them were dancing together that Lucy, idle at the side of the room, was struck by the girl's appearance.

Louisa wore her same white muslin with the glossy spots and, although her dancing was now graceful and her looks improved recently so that she was almost pretty, it was her whole manner that caught Lucy's notice: Louisa had the serene glow of a girl in love. Lucy's acuteness could not fail to recognise it. So then, Lucy wondered, what can the man be waiting for? She determined to do what she could to hasten the matter along. Her own *ennui* wanted something to happen, increased as it was by this evening's tedium. It was proper to attend a ball under one's sister's chaperonage and accompanied only by friends, but that made the occasion the more tedious, when so many attractive strangers might have been encountered. Lucy was next asked to dance by Mr Forgan himself.

"I hope," he said, "that you are enjoying the evening more

than your expression might suggest."

She allowed her expression to deny his hope, and replied: "Certain persons are happy to be here, I notice."

"You refer to myself? I admit that I am fond of dancing."

"I referred to other certain persons also." She was looking at Louisa who, without a partner, sat in contented reverie by the wall. Mr Forgan, wondering, following her gaze; his own expression softened.

"You refer, perhaps, to Miss Retford? Yes, she is charming tonight. I fancy she is become more at ease in gatherings such as this, even during the last few weeks. I fancy too that she may owe that to your own encouragement and guidance."

"To mine, rather than to my sister's?" asked Lucy with an archness that made him, after an interval of pretending not to understand her, yield a rueful smile.

"Miss Steele has proved a delightful and – entertaining friend, and I am glad to have made her acquaintance."

"Well, if you value my encouragement and guidance for yourself as well as for Louisa, you may take it from me that you need not pursue the acquaintance further."

"I do not understand you?" He truly seemed at a loss.

"I mean that, if you intend to approach Miss Retford, you should do so direct. I judge the approach would be acceptable, and I see no reason for delay."

Mr Forgan absorbed this advice without resentment. He was thoughtful for a while, then said: "You have divined my feelings. I did not think I had made them obvious. I am sure you are as discreet as you are perceptive, and so I will trespass on your attention to describe my motives in what you see as delay. As I have just remarked to you, Miss Retford is only now becoming accustomed to society, and undergoing many new experiences; some of her own feelings may be strange to her."

"She is growing up, that is all," said Lucy in summary.

"Quite so. She is very young. For that reason, one hesitates to ask her for a lifelong decision. At the same time she has, for one so young, a well-formed mind of her own. It would be no small thing to gain her complete confidence. She would not be easily swept off her feet."

"Even by charm such as yours," said Lucy.

Mr Forgan laughed. "Your flattery implies only that I flatter myself. Miss Retford, to be serious, would not be susceptible to flattery, or to any ill-contrived approach. Shall I tell you," he added in a confidential tone, "my secret plan? I am not as dilatory as you think, or only for a reason that you may think insufficient. However, this is what I had designed: Some time ago, I suggested a sailing party, to which I could invite all my friends. This would necessitate the hire of a sizable boat, and it is partly there that the delay arises; until the height of summer, such boats are not to be obtained. At the end of next week, if the weather permits, my party should take place. We would sail across the bay, and land for a picnic on the island at the tip of the far promontory; you may have seen it from here, on a clear day. It is very pretty, with tamarisk trees and pools and pathways where one may wander about. It was there that I hoped to wander with Miss Retford, arrange that we had some moments alone, and make my proposal. Am I being absurdly romantic?"

"I do not suspect you of any such weakness. Moreover, your plan will allow Louisa one more week in which to become less young," said Lucy, unable to doubt his sincerity or to find fault with his project.

"I must beg you, although I know I need not, to say no word of any of this to Miss Retford?"

Lucy assured him that she would drop no hint to Louisa; she did not promise, however, to keep the secret from Nancy, and was glad that Mr Forgan omitted to require discretion in that direction. Now that she was informed of Mr Forgan's intentions, Lucy had a weapon that she might, or might not, use against her sister; her evening had not been entirely unprofitable, after all.

10

The two days following the ball were rainy; on the third morning, although the clouds were breaking, the weather was not encouraging to walks on the promenade nor with Miss King; as there was no Latin lesson, Louisa announced that she would visit Mrs Benson.

"Oh, please, take me with you!" pleaded George. "Mrs Benson might tell us the way to the smugglers' caves!"

"Be quiet, George. You are going to no caves," said Lucy.

"No, ma'am."

Louisa set off alone, in a light drizzle that soon ceased; when she reached Quay Street the cobbles were steaming in rays of sun. Mrs Benson welcomed her, brought out the cowslip wine, and asked after Mr Retford, and about Louisa's activities, but in a manner that lacked her previous openness. It was apparent that something troubled her, cordial though she wished to be; and presently Louisa asked: "Mrs Benson, are you not feeling well? Shall I leave you?"

"No, no. I am quite well. That is – I am glad to see you. Please forgive me if I am distracted. Do go on with your tale of the ball. You danced with Mr King ...?"

"Yes," took up Louisa, doubtful that this recital could entertain anyone, distracted or not. "Then I danced with Mr Forgan, and –" She broke off, because Mrs Benson had twisted her hands together and pursed her mouth as if in sudden pain. "I am sure you are not well, nor do you wish to hear my chattering. Can I help you in any way?"

"Oh, no, it is good of you, and I like to hear you talk. It is just that I am in such a difficulty – Miss Retford, there is one thing you might be able to tell me: how long is Mr Forgan to stay in Brightsea?"

"I do not know," said Louisa in some surprise. "Has he not visited you again?"

At this, Mrs Benson covered her face with her apron and moaned: "Oh, I do not know *what* to do ..."

"I beg you, tell me your trouble," Louisa urged, with a concern that affected Mrs Benson, who shook her head, but lowered her apron and wound it into a bundle as she slowly said:

"I cannot speak of it to anyone. But I owe it to you, Miss Retford, to warn you against Mr Forgan. I have understood that he has been paying attention to you, and if you are fond of him I am very sorry, and will not interfere; but I owe it too to your grandfather, dear Mr Retford, who would want me to set you on your guard. What is more, it was I who brought it on you, by answering his questions when he had passed you on my doorstep. I told him of your family, and your circumstances, and I should have known better, but I did not mean to gossip, and seeing him in my house made me so upset I hardly knew what I was saying, and even then, it was when he came the next time that he – Oh, dear, I cannot believe what he did, but it could have been no one else."

Louisa, a little confused, asked: "What can you have told Mr Forgan of my circumstances?"

"Oh, just that you are heiress to Mr Retford, and will be very rich."

"I suppose I shall. I had not thought of it. And that is what has made Mr Forgan friendly?" She reflected, and added: "I remember that I did think it strange, that he suddenly introduced himself to us. But it was my companion, Miss Steele, whom he seemed to prefer."

"So you yourself do not ... are not attached to him?"

"No, though he is pleasant, and I enjoy his conversation."

"Pleasant he can be," cried Mrs Benson. "I am glad to know that whatever else he has done, he has not broken your heart."

Louisa thought of Miss King, with a qualm, but pursued: "What do you mean by 'whatever else'? What has Mr Forgan done?"

Mrs Benson smoothed out her crumpled apron, then crumpled it again, before evidently coming to a decision. "Miss Retford, I will tell you my story, for the relief of it, and because I know you are a kind soul – lady, I mean – and will tell no one else. You must be a little patient, because it goes back more than two years, to the time when I was nurse to poor Mrs Forgan. I was over three months in the house before she passed away, poor lady, and so I knew how things went with them. You know that she was of very good family, and had money, and he spent it all. When I was there, it was nothing but rack and ruin, that beautiful house, because poor Mrs Forgan could not leave her bed, so he took no care of anything but was in and out with his pleasures and his smart clothes, and tradesmen lacking their money – You know how servants will talk" (and, Louisa was not sophisticated enough to add, nurses will listen) "so I knew what he was like; with his poor wife dying, he was half his time in London, and it was as well for her she was so ill, she never realised how cruel he was. Well, when she passed away, poor Mrs Forgan, he had spent all her money already, but, much worse than that, while she was so ill he had taken all her jewellery and sold it. Can you credit such wickedness? Now, because you see her family was so important, there was some jewellery that was by way of being heirlooms, as well as valuable. So when her family – chiefly it was her uncle, Lord Marchendale – came to reclaim what was theirs, since it belonged in the family, poor Mrs Forgan having no children, what did Mr Forgan find to say except that it had all been stolen. Now, Lord Marchendale and the others, knowing already what Mr

Forgan was like, did not believe him. I was gone from the house by then, you see, but I heard of it all through a friend who had gone to nurse a poor lady who was niece to Lady Marchendale. Well, so I thought, I hope they punish him as a common thief, let alone for all the lies he has told, and I heard he had to sell the house, not that the money would keep him long if he did not alter his ways: and I thought I had seen the last of him. But no; it seems the family would not give up, in this quest for the jewellery back, and they have been after him ever since. And now, this is where I am unlucky enough to come into the story again. This year, Mr Forgan finds me out, and comes here to say he must discover who stole the jewels. Can you credit such impudence? He said it was probably someone who was in the house during poor Mrs Forgan's last days, and he tried to have me name a footman, Alfred his name was, such a nice young man and honest as the day; but when he left the house, without his own pay too like most of them, well, Alfred went as a sailor, and very soon his ship was sunk, which we all heard of. Mr Forgan said to me: "Mrs Benson, you will remember you never trusted Alfred." And I said I remembered no such thing. So then, he talked of Lady Forgan's maid, Cicely; and he said, if I could remember who the thief must be, and be ready to say so to the Marchendales, he would pay me money. Now there is a word for that sort of thing, Miss Retford, and it is a word I do not like. So when he had gone on for a while I finally said: 'Mr Forgan, I was in poor Mrs Forgan's room for most of my time, and I remember very well who it was who came and took one thing after another from her jewel box, saying it was for safe keeping, or to have it cleaned for when the poor lady was better, or some such tale.' So after that, he went off, very angry, and I was angry myself." Indignation had coloured Mrs Benson's face as she spoke, but now she paused, sighed, and resumed in a shaking voice:

"I want to show you now, Miss Retford, what it is that has put me in such trouble. It was only yesterday morning.

Do you see, here I keep my workbasket." Standing, Mrs Benson shook out her apron and crossed to the dresser, bringing a large workbasket which she set on the stool by Louisa's chair. "Now yesterday in the morning, I suddenly thought to send my granddaughter my grandmother's silver thimble, which I had meant to send for a christening present, but somehow I forgot. So, you see, under the sewing ... and my bobbins on their box ..." Emptying the basket carefully, Mrs Benson revealed at the bottom a small parcel made of a silk kerchief. "In here, are a few treasures that I never look at. Why I thought of the thimble, I shall never know. This is the ring my husband, poor Mr Benson, bought me at Cockermouth fair when we were courting ... the ribbon of my little girl's first shoe ... a pebble from the Sea of Galilee, that perhaps Our Lord trod upon – it was given to me by a cousin who made a pilgrimage ... and *this*." Mrs Benson's tone as she laid out her treasures had been reverent, but as she held out the last object she spoke with terse disgust. Louisa saw a pendant, of gold, ornamented with chips of garnet.

"Who gave you that?" she ventured.

"Why, do you not understand? *He*. Mr Forgan hid it in my basket. Who else? I was surprised, that when I offered him my cowslip wine he asked instead for some buttermilk. But out I went to the pantry, and it took me some mintues to prepare it. But, Miss Retford, why did he put that pendant in my basket?"

The reason as it suggested itself to Louisa horrified her. "Does he mean ... is this one of the missing jewels?"

"See, on the back, is the lion with the two oak leaves, engraved. That is the coat of arms of the Marchendales. Miss Retford, what am I to do? Who is supposed to discover this, and why has no one yet come?"

"What you are to do," said Louisa with decision, "is to have the pendant removed from your house at once. I shall take it with me." She dropped the pendant into her carrying bag and pulled its strings firmly shut. "And the next thing, is to search all through the house, to make sure nothing else has been hidden."

"Oh, my dear Miss Retford, I thought of that, and since yesterday I have been through the house so that not a pin could I have overlooked. Oh, what a relief, if you would take the pendant away. It is not of great value, but I dare not throw it away. What will you do with it?"

"I shall think about that. Let it be a comfort for the present, that you cannot now be accused. It may be that the Marchendales have not yet caught up with Mr Forgan at Brightsea, or are at least not harrying him at the moment. Now, let your mind be at rest, and do not let Mr Forgan into your house again."

It did not occur to Louisa to doubt Mrs Benson, mostly because it did not occur to Mrs Benson that she would not be believed. Mrs Benson's gratitude was such that she kissed Louisa with tears as they parted; and Louisa as she walked home thought only of Mrs Benson's predicament, and her good fortune in happening to look out that thimble yesterday. In her room, Louisa dropped the pendant into her own jewel box; she had never desired jewellery, and the only items in the box she valued were a pearl necklace that had belonged to her mother, and a necklace of sea-shells that Jenny had helped George and Augusta to make on a wet day. Othewise, she possessed only an assortment of trinkets given to her by school friends. She closed the lid of the box as if putting an end to a difficulty, and only then did she recollect Mr Forgan, whom she must still meet with her knowledge of his perfidy in mind. To have delivered Mrs Benson from a difficulty had delivered Louisa into one of her own.

She believed what Mrs Benson had told her, but was incredulous that Mr Forgan could be capable of thievery and deceit. Such conduct showed a cheap and repulsive nature quite out of accord with what Louisa had known of his. How could a gentleman of Mr Forgan's manners and taste neglect a dying wife, rob her, and try to implicate others? Louisa was bewildered. What was more, she did not feel at all easy to be possessed of such disturbing knowledge; was it in any way her duty to mention it to anyone else; should Miss King, for example, be warned that she was in danger of bestowing her affections in such an unworthy direction? Louisa wished she had Miss Worthington to advise her. But, struggling to compose herself, she recollected: this evening we are to have the card party only here; it is not until tomorrow that I shall have to face him.

Face Mr Forgan, even after a day's respite, Louisa could not. The ladies from Stanley Crescent were invited to the house taken by some friends of Mr King's, recently arrived in the town. This family had several daughters, the house was spacious, so there was to be dancing, for which every available partner had been summoned. Mr Forgan was prompt to greet Miss Steele and to agree with her admiration of her dress, and to bow to Mrs Ferrars with an uneffusive compliment on her complexion; but before he could turn to Louisa she had escaped, pretending to be in haste to find Miss King. The sound of his voice had thrown Louisa into such agitation that she could not look at him. When he asked her to dance she could not raise her eyes to his, and at the touch of his hand her own shrank away. The strangeness of her demeanour could not but strike him. Presently he asked:

"Are you not feeling well this evening?"

"I am well, sir," Louisa replied in so subdued a voice that he must bend his head to hear her.

"Then," he said in a gentle tone, "has something made you unhappy?"

She shook her head, blushing and speechless.

"Come, I am sure you are not in good health or spirits, and for the sake of either, would you not prefer to sit down, and let me bring you a glass of wine?"

Louisa shook her head and nodded it, anxious only to be away from him, and, seeing Mrs Ferrars nearby on a sofa, with less than a murmur of excuse left the set and fled to her side. Mr Forgan followed, solicitous, to suggest that Miss Retford might wish to be taken home? Mrs Ferrars asked what was wrong with Miss Retford and Louisa, her cheeks still deeply coloured, protested in a whisper that nothing was wrong.

"She was in excellent health all today," stated Mrs Ferrars. "You had better leave her alone, Mr Forgan, until the occasion of our island picnic."

Mr Forgan bowed and walked away, a not implausible suspicion forming itself in his mind. For the rest of that evening he did not approach either Louisa or Mrs Ferrars, nor did his face reflect the merriment that gained on the rest of the company, especially when Signor Jacomo took over the pianoforte and played country dances with such verve and buoyancy that everyone leapt tirelessly to and fro.

On the next morning Louisa accompanied Miss Steele on some shopping, then they joined Mrs Ferrars on the terrace of the Spring Pavilion. In hot summer weather this walk made a change from the promenade and was as pleasant, the paved way bordered as it was with flowering shrubs and hedges curved into alcoves. "Even here, it grows crowded," Mrs Ferrars complained. "There is that portly Mrs Yarrow – let us avoid her. I wonder she does not despair of bringing her drunken son to heel. And here comes Mr Forgan. Why is he here? I do not suppose he drinks the waters."

At the mention of that name, Louisa had made an involuntary movement as if to turn aside, and Miss Steele, not listening to her sister, and feeling the heat of the flagstones, turned after Louisa; they made for a bench in an alcove of the hedge, and Mrs Ferrars came with them. Mr Forgan, however, was already near enough to say to her:

"Good morning to you, Mrs Ferrars. It is urgent that I speak to you alone. Would you grant me a few moments?"

"Very well," consented Lucy, turning back. The two of them walked off for some paces, and Louisa thankfully settled herself on the bench. Miss Steele, instead of seating herself, stood peering round the hedge corner and muttering:

"Why should he speak to Lucy alone? What can he have private to say? La! They are gone too far off, I cannot hear. I declare, they are in the next curve of the hedge, sitting on a bench, whispering secrets. See, here at this corner the hedge is thin; I can go through it, and behind, and hear what they are saying."

"Miss Steele," cried Louisa, in dismay and reproof, "you cannot mean to listen – you will tear your gown –"

"Oh, Louisa, hush, they will hear you. Hold my parasol, and you must say I was here with you all the time," Miss Steele adjured her, while scrambling her way through the hedge corner. Passing along behind the hedge she could observe through its next angle that her sister and Mr Forgan had indeed entered another alcove, where they were not sitting on the bench, but standing, while Mr Forgan said in an earnest tone:

"... You promise me, then, that you have said nothing to her?"

"Not a word. Why should I have?"

"But her manner to me last evening was so much changed, I must suppose something has disturbed her. Perhaps your sister has committed some indiscretion?"

"Nancy has committed a thousand indiscretions," allowed Lucy in an indifferent voice, "but she would have told me had she meddled in this affair, for she is indiscreet enough always to boast of them."

Mr Forgan uttered an irritable exclamation that covered from him and Lucy a muffled exclamation from behind the hedge. "She has not spoken of me since yesterday evening, then?" he resumed.

"Nancy? Possibly she has; I forget."

"Miss Retford," corrected Mr Forgan with an effort of patience. "You can give me no guidance, on how I should proceed?"

"Except that you should proceed, no."

"I apologise for troubling you. But I thank you for what reassurance you can give me, negative as it may be." The valedictory note of this reminded Miss Steele that she was supposed to be at some distance away, and she hurried to burst through the hedge again and sit, breathless and with twigs of leaves stuck in her bonnet, beside Louisa, before Lucy could return, which Lucy immediately did.

While gaining her breath and an air of innocence Miss Steel realised that, in Louisa's presence, she had better not demand the meaning of the overheard conversation. As soon as she was alone with her sister at home, she did not hesitate to begin:

"I know that you and Mr Forgan hid yourselves away to say unkind things of me, but I am sure he would not believe you, for he has been my admirer this ever so long, since before you came here, which I wish you never had —" And she was about to proceed by asking why Mr Forgan spoke of Louisa, but Lucy took the opportunity of attacking:

"Good God, Nancy, so do I; and I wish too you would stop being such a fool, in pretending you have admirers, when you are long past the age for that sort of thing, and indeed had any man ever admired you, you would have been married years ago. It is like your silly conceit, to imagine Mr Forgan and I should speak of you. Far from being a beau of yours," she added, "Mr Forgan proposes to marry Louisa."

"Yes, that is what I —" But Miss Steele checked herself before admitting that she had deduced as much from behind the hedge. She rallied and went on: "I do not know why you should think I considered Mr Forgan as a husband, if that is what you are hinting, in your spite. He is a fine man, and whatever you say, he is among my admirers, but la! I have others, though you are too jealous to admit it, discontented as you are with your own lot, with your quarrelling Robert and all that stuck-up family. Mr Forgan, forsooth! He is younger than me — Well, by a little — and has not even a house of his own as far as one knows.

He may do very well for Louisa, for they will have her money, and her grandfather will be pleased that while she is in my charge I have found her a handsome husband and settled her so early in life."

If it were Miss Steele's conceit which inspired this speech, she had nevertheless adjusted herself to the situation in a superb fashion. Lucy, disappointed perhaps, said no more, but left the room with a gesture of disdain, while Miss Steele remained to soothe her own disappointment in private, and review the future with a revival of optimism. Lucy's insults she disregarded; Lucy had always made the worst of anything that concerned Nancy.

Probably, Miss Steele inferred, Mr Forgan had not yet spoken to Louisa, or the happy news would have been reported. In no doubt that the news would be happy, Miss Steele did not suppose either that the matter was a secret, though she did not yet speak of it to Louisa. She began to make her own dispositions.

A first result of these was that Mr Dwyer, arriving next morning for a Latin lesson, found Miss Steele dressed and curled and established with her carpetwork in the drawing-room. "Good morning to you, Mr Dwyer," she cried in her most cheerful voice. "I am afraid I have been neglecting my duties of late, and not sitting as chaperone at your lesson. I hope I am forgiven."

"Certainly," Mr Dwyer answered in faint surprise. "We have, however, had the pleasure of Master George's chaperonage." He laid his hand on the head of George, who had come running into the room when he heard Mr Dwyer's arrival.

"Oh, George has no business with you, George, be off, and go to Jenny in the back parlour, as your mother says you must."

"Yes, ma'am," said George, with reluctance.

As soon as George had withdrawn Miss Steele said: "Miss Dwyer is recovered, I hear? Then I hope you will be more free yourself to come into company. I suppose you do not go to balls?"

"I do not often have the opportunity."

"Well, in Brightsea you would have it, if you can dance."

"Yes, ma'am; I enjoy dancing."

"Oh, that is splendid. Then you must come to the ball next week. Miss Dwyer will spare you for one evening. I shall present you to some of my friends. There are some pretty girls among them. But I shall not present you to too many, lest I lose all your attention. Lord, how I shall be wondered at, standing up with a clergyman! But you do not look like one, you know. Our vicar in London, Mr Pewitt, is such an inconsiderable little man. But you must not think I think ill of your cloth. We have clergymen among our relations. And I might have thought Louisa would marry a clergyman, it would suit her quite well, except that she is to marry Mr Forgan."

Mr Dwyer, who had been quietly laying out his books on the table, now raised his head and stared at her astonished. "Miss Retford is to marry Mr Forgan?"

"Oh, we have not yet announced it, but it is more or less decided, and he has spoken to my sister – that is, to me, because I am in charge of her, and I was glad to give him permission to ask for her hand, and I am sure she favours him, as indeed what young lady would not."

"I hope they will both be very happy," said Mr Dwyer, closing one of his books and then opening it again.

"Oh, you can be sure of that."

Louisa now entered the room. She had been detained by meeting George in the hallway and consoling him over his banishment, and had been hoping that Miss Steele too would leave; but she perceived now that Miss Steele intended to stay, and took her place at the table. Mr Dwyer, had he studied her, might not have imagined that he beheld a young lady who was sure to be very happy. Louisa's face was pale and she was evidently troubled. Mr Dwyer, however, was himself cooler in his manner than usual, and drew Louisa's attention at once to the chapter of Caesar that he had prepared for her construing.

The lesson continued soberly, interrupted only by a few remarks from Miss Steele upon the state of the weather and of her carpetwork. In her presence, and the absence of George, tutor and pupil would in any case not have been on their usual terms, but Louisa could sense that Mr Dwyer was at a new distance from her. He was as gentle and patient as ever, but did not smile; even, when she had made a mistake in translation, it was she who noticed it before he had, and corrected it with an apology.

"I am sorry," Mr Dwyer apologised in turn. "That was unobservant of me."

"Why, we cannot have unobservant gentlemen about us!" exclaimed Miss Steele from across the room. It nettled her that neither of the others accorded any observation to her exclamation either.

Louisa was the more saddened, because she had during a restless night formed the resolution of consulting Mr Dwyer about Mr Forgan. She had wondered that such an idea had not occurred to her sooner, because she trusted entirely in Mr Dwyer's wisdom and discretion, and besides, the thought of confiding in Mr Dwyer tempted her; noting the temptation, she had denied herself the anticipation of any pleasure in seeking his advice; but, preparing herself to make her appeal in an impersonal fashion, she had been less than prepared to find Mr Dwyer as impersonal as she. This morning, she dared not imagine even that she could visit his house, an expedient that would hitherto have rid them of the interventions of Miss Steele. At the end of the hour, Mr Dwyer and Louisa took leave of each other with a formality that showed no chaperonage of the lessons to have been at all necessary; if the formality on both sides concealed sadness, both had the strength of mind to conceal it.

11

James Forgan had no idea of himself as a common thief, and was indignant that the Marchendales dared threaten to treat him as such, by accusing him of making off with the family jewels. As they persisted in this vulgar attitude, he came to see that he must clear himself; this could be done only by retrieving the jewellery and pretending to have found it hidden somewhere; or by inculpating someone else.

To retrieve the jewellery he would need a great deal of money. For a great deal of money, one needed, as he had previously proved, a rich wife. James Forgan was assiduous in his search for one. His old friend Luigi Jacomo promised that the jewels might be, at a price, recovered; it was Luigi who had undertaken to dispose of them, safely abroad, through an unscrupulous merchant he knew in Milan. James Forgan would rather have enjoyed inculpating Luigi, but, unluckily, Luigi had been out of the country during the time that the thefts had taken place, and could be implicated as no more than an accomplice. Luigi, little help as he at present was, must besides be kept as an ally, lest his good offices be needed with the Milan merchant. James Forgan did not care to be thus dependent on anyone, but could not help it in the case of Luigi, who had been privy to the operation from its outset, and whose discretion James Forgan was compelled to rely on; which he did, if only because Luigi took nothing about it seriously.

Luigi Jacomo was dedicated to music. Such principles as he had were confined too to that. He was deeply shocked by a wrong note played or sung, but found the larcenous transactions of his friend James Forgan merely amusing. It suited him to accept invitations to James Forgan's rich friends while he was in England; promising to regain the jewellery, he omitted to mention that many of the gold items that bore the Marchendale coat of arms had already been melted down. It was he who advised James Forgan to use the pendant with the garnets, and the coat of arms on its back, as indication of guilt, and to dispose of any other of the smaller jewels that he had not thought worth taking to Milan. He approved his friend's choice of an old ex-nurse as recipient of the incriminating pendant, and approved James Forgan's pursuit of Miss Retford as a second wife, without concerning himself with the fate of either of the ladies. Meanwhile he was passing a pleasant summer at Brightsea, occasionally travelling to London on his musical business, and in no hurry that James Forgan's should be completed.

Nor had James Forgan been in a great hurry; Lord Marchendale had left the affair of the theft in the hands of his solicitors, from whom dilatoriness can always be expected, and gone for some months to the south of France. With the pendant concealed in Mrs Benson's cottage, developments could be awaited, while court was paid to Miss Retford. This process James Forgan had initiated as soon as Mrs Benson told him of Miss Retford's expectations – which, as she had only a delicate old grandfather, might be expected very soon – and he had been satisfied with its progress, until the interference of those two sisters, the acute Mrs Ferrars and the stupid Miss Steele, appeared to be forcing the issue.

How this had come about, Mr Forgan could not ascertain, but he was disturbed. The consciousness that he had lately noticed in Louisa he could not identify as revulsion, shyness, or a suppressed new awareness of him; he was not reassured by his conversation with Mrs Ferrars in the Pavilion gardens; he could not now be content to wait for his sailing trip and the romantic setting of the island. He consulted Luigi Jacomo, who was studying the score of an oratorio.

"Luigi, what is she feeling towards me? There has been a change. I cannot understand her, but I must make some contact, lest I lose her –"

Signor Jacomo looked over his eyeglasses to say: "If those aunts of hers have been talking, it is no wonder she has changed." He made a mark on the score with his pen.

"They are not her aunts ... Why, then, should she change?"

"Because she now waits for you to speak."

"Should I do so?"

"Oh, yes, I should," said Signor Jacomo, writing.

This was very much what Mr Forgan had wanted to be told. He prepared himself for a call at the house in Stanley Crescent, walking thither in sunshine and renewed confidence. He had come to admire and respect Miss Retford, dull and childish as he had at first thought her, and of late, since Mrs Ferrars first spoke to him, had observed in her many of the signs of a young girl in love. He looked back now to that encouragement, and looked forward to the resolution of Miss Retford's trouble and her delight in receiving his declaration.

Louisa was in the back parlour, playing at snake-in-the-grass with George and Augusta while Jenny gossiped with Molly in the kitchen. When John came in to say: "Miss Retford, Mr Forgan has called," she said:

"Then show him into the drawing-room, John, and bring Miss Steele or Mrs Ferrars to him. I am occupied here."

"It is you he wishes to see, Miss, and Mrs Ferrars said I was to send you in."

Louisa did not in the least wish to see Mr Forgan, but with John standing to hold the door for her she could summon no quick excuse, nor did she feel it prudent to set the children an example of disobedience to Mrs Ferrars. Straightening her hair and dress as she rose from the floor, she went to the drawing-room, and was disconcerted to find

Mr Forgan alone there; she had supposed Mrs Ferrars present. Louisa paused in the doorway, as if ready to flee, and Mr Forgan stepped forward as if to prevent her.

"I must beg you," he said, "to hear what I have to say." What that might be, Louisa was less than prepared to imagine. His smile was at its most pleasant; she could almost doubt his villainy. But when she understood what he had to say, she was so much in doubt that he could truly wish to marry her, that she could only stand silent, amazed; doubts returned, reflected from those of her own unworthiness upon her secret knowledge of his. In her amazement she was not entirely just to Mr Forgan, who did sincerely mean to ask for her hand; Louisa had never yet anticipated that anyone would wish to marry her. His offer rendered the whole position more incredible, and no more comfortable. When he ceased speaking, and waited with a questioning smile, she after struggling for breath could say only, in a tremulous voice:

"No, sir. I cannot marry you."

Mr Forgan was visibly taken aback. "But why not?" he asked, with a startled abruptness.

"You must not make me ... explain," murmured Louisa.

"But indeed, explanation is due to me."

Even in her confusion, Louisa sensed the house silent behind her as if it were listening, and she remembered Miss Steele behind the hedge in the Pavilion gardens. She moved forward into the room and closed the door. She felt nothing due to Mr Forgan from her, but courage required that she confront him. She said:

"I am afraid, Mr Forgan, I have not a high regard for your character."

"I am sorry to hear that," he replied, still smiling, as if tolerating some whim of a child's. "I had not guessed that you were sitting in judgement upon my character, during our very agreeable association."

Louisa's literal and exact type of mind compelled her to admit: "You have been kind to me. I enjoyed our association, until I came to know how it was that you had behaved to other people."

"Indeed? Perhaps you should enlarge upon this regrettable behaviour."

"I had much rather not discuss it, Mr Forgan."

"But it would be a kindness to me," he said, his tone still mild, "to tell me what evil reports have reached you. It is painful to find oneself subject to calumny."

"Then … I know that you – took possessions that did not belong to you, and tried to shed the blame for it on innocent people."

"And you believed such an extraordinary story? I am not flattered. Might I ask from whom you heard it?"

Louisa for the first time raised her eyes to him. He seemed very tall, and she felt very small as he towered over her. She clenched her hands behind her back, but said with firmness:

"You must have guessed that it was Mrs Benson."

Mr Forgan laughed. "Oh yes, it must have been that old woman in the lower village. I am sorry to have to tell you that, when she was in my employment, I did not find her honest. I am sorry too that she has been passing on her fables to you. I have done what I can to make her more comfortable in her old age, but from such a person one does not expect gratitude. I am a little surprised, however, that she should display her ingratitude by spreading slanders of me; and I am surprised also that you, Miss Retford, should believe her. Let us put her out of mind, and let my character be restored in your eyes, that we may be friends again, and soon become more than that."

Louisa found him so persuasive, and his authority so powerful, that it took all her innate obstinacy to force her to reply:

"But, Mr Forgan, I do believe Mrs Benson."

His smile was pitying. "Yes, I know, she is very plausible in her speech; and you, after all, are very young."

Very young, as well as very small, Louisa felt as she faced

him. Yet she knew that she was right, and he wrong. Suddenly, she remembered:

"Mrs Benson gave me the pendant. I have it upstairs."

"A pendant?" repeated Mr Forgan in polite inquiry.

"The pendant that you hid in her workbasket." As he gazed at her with raised eyebrows, shaking his head to show ignorance, she added: "Wait. I will show you."

She hurried out of the room, almost surprising Miss Steele, the flutter of whose skirt vanished behind the door of the opposite room as Louisa emerged. Unnoticing, Louisa ran up the stairs and to her jewel box. She searched it, and then emptied its contents across the bed and sorted each piece apart; then she sought in the drawer from which she had taken the jewel box, and about her dressing-table and cupboards, but to no effect. She knew perfectly that she had put the pendant in her jewel box. Now it was not to be found.

She went more slowly downstairs again. Mr Forgan, as requested, was waiting. She told him:

"The pendant is no longer there."

"No, I suppose not. Now, dear Miss Retford, will you relinquish your game of make-believe and admit your mistake?"

"No," answered Louisa in simple refusal.

"I will overlook your fantastic accusations," Mr Forgan told her, "and attribute your behaviour to some girlish freak. We shall say no more of Mrs Benson and stolen heirlooms. Nor, if you are prudent, will you repeat such tales further, lest you be taken for as great a liar as she. Let me assure you of my continued regard. We shall meet again soon, I hope on an easier occasion. Please give my compliments to Miss Steele and Mrs Ferrars." He bowed and left the room and, as Louisa could hear, went directly out of the house.

She sat at, almost fell onto, the table and laid her head on a book while tears fell on to its cover. The various shocks of the last half-hour threatened now to overwhelm her. She thought: "Oh, Mr Dwyer, what shall I do?" Recollection of that name reminded her that it was on a book of his that her head rested, and she drew herself upright. The book was Mr Dwyer's *Caesar*, and tears had washed off spots of colour from its binding, leaving white marks that nothing would obliterate; when Louisa rubbed at them with her fingers, in fact, her finger became stained with red dye. This distraction served to check her tears and free her mind a little and she began to reflect on her interview with Mr Forgan. She had to admit that, in the absence of the pendant, she had no plaint against Mr Forgan; her education had trained her to place proof above supposition: without evidence, one had no case. As she recalled their conversation she remembered: "He said we would say no more of 'Mrs Benson and stolen heirlooms'. But I had said nothing of heirlooms. My own words were: 'You took *possessions* that did not belong to you.' This reassured Louisa herself, but would not convince anyone who heard Mr Forgan's account of the words if it differed from her own.

Only one thought that followed did cheer her: Mr Forgan had parted from her in a cool manner and without returning to the question of marriage. "And surely after what passed between us," Louisa concluded, "he cannot have any more idea of that."

If this conclusion comforted Louisa, it did not please Mrs Ferrars, who after allowing Louisa a little time for private felicity, now came into the drawing-room with her own felicitations ready. Mrs Ferrar's immediate reaction was of horror when she saw Louisa's face, not radiant with joy, but streaked with blood. "My dear Louisa," she cried, "what have you been doing, to have blood all over your face?"

Louisa looked down at her fingers, with which she had wiped her tears off her cheeks, to the liberal distribution of their red dye. She realised what had happened and said:

"It is Mr Dwyer's –"

"Mr Dwyer's blood?" cried Miss Steele in turn, hastening in after her sister.

"No – it is from the book –"

"You must wash your face then," said Lucy with a confirmatory glance at the smeared *Caesar*, "but before all, Louisa, I must say how happy I am."

"I am glad, ma'am. Why are you happy?"

"Well, because you and Mr Forgan are engaged, of course."

"But we are not."

"Not? After I stepped aside for your sake?" exclaimed Miss Steele.

"Be quiet, Nancy – You did not refuse him, Louisa?"

"Yes. I did."

"But why, in heaven's name?"

Louisa had not anticipated that she must give her reasons over again for her refusal, but she said:

"I do not hold Mr Forgan in high esteem."

She pronounced this with a finality that provoked both her hearers. They could not know that, after her encounter with Mr Forgan, no further encounter could for the moment frighten her; her exhausted nerves gave her manner the quality of calm obstinacy. Nor could Louisa see why Miss Steele should be so aghast or Mrs Ferrars so angry.

"High esteem?" echoed Mrs Ferrars, incredulous. "And pray, who are you to deny your *esteem* to such a man?"

"And what has that to do with not marrying him?" demanded Miss Steele.

"You must reconsider. Very well, he may have surprised you with his declaration, but you are too young and inexperienced to decide in such a hurry," Mrs Ferrars insisted. Her pride was touched, that Louisa should have failed what had been virtually a promise on her behalf from Mrs Ferrars to Mr Forgan. "I am disappointed in you, Louisa; you show yourself headstrong and impulsive. You must be guided by me –"

"And me," put in Miss Steele.

"– And when Mr Forgan renews his offer, I shall expect a different outcome."

"He will not renew his offer, ma'am."

"How do you know that? Upon my word, you take far too much on yourself. There is a sneaking stubbornness in you that I have never liked. You fancy yourself clever, but you cannot set up your judgement against that of older and wiser people. You have no idea of the ways of the world –"

"Nor of dressing yourself to appear in it," added Miss Steele.

"And whatever it is that you hold against Mr Forgan, it is a creation of your own bookish conceit, I am sure of that. What is it that you have against him?"

Louisa hesitated for a moment, then said: "I cannot explain."

"Well then, it can be nothing of importance. You do not know your own mind, which is a consequence of so much education, which in practice leads only to ignorance. Do not stand there looking so mulish – and so ugly, with those stains on your face. Go and wash them off." And as Louisa, thankful to be dismissed, quitted the room, Mrs Ferrars called after her: "We shall soon break down your selfish obduracy. You have not heard the last of this."

Nor, indeed, had she. The recriminations continued, and the whole household was rendered disturbed and uncomfortable. George and Augusta, sensing that Louisa was in disgrace, peeped at her shyly; Louisa was not allowed to be alone, but must listen to harangues from Mrs Ferrars and Miss Steele alternately; that Louisa had nothing to say in answer, deepened the impression of her obstinacy, and that this was so often pointed out to her increased her wretchedness.

Mr Forgan, as Louisa had expected, did not call again on that day. The next morning she was bidden to accompany Miss Steele to the milliner's since, there, they were unlikely to meet him. They happened, however, to meet Miss King, who greeted Louisa in a friendlier way than she had for some time. Clasping Louisa's hand and drawing her aside, Miss King said:

"My dear Miss Retford, my aunt has told me in confidence – and Mr Forgan told her in confidence, so you must not say I told you – that he made you an offer of marriage, and that you refused him!"

"That is true," agreed Louisa.

"I wonder at that," said Miss King with a brilliant smile. "And how did he take his refusal? Was he much cast down?"

"I do not know. I think not."

"I dare say your friends were surprised that you refused him?"

"They are angry," Louisa confessed. "They say I should have accepted his offer."

"Well, and if you did not, I am sure you did the right thing. It would be very unwise to accept a man unless you truly loved him. You do not think you will change your mind? You truly have no affection for him?"

"No, I have none," replied Louisa with a sincerity that caused Miss King's smile to become brighter still. This meeting did nothing to raise Louisa's spirits; she was certain that Miss King should not entrust her own affections to a man of Mr Forgan's character, but had not the courage or the unkindness to say so; and, besides, Miss King like everyone else would not believe her story of his wickedness.

"What was Miss King saying to you?" asked Miss Steele as soon as Miss King had left.

"She has heard from Mrs King that I refused Mr Forgan's proposal."

"La! Is he telling the whole town? I would have expected more tact of him. Let us hope it does not mean he gives you up." Miss Steele hastened with this hope to Mrs Ferrars, whose own hopes on the case were not sanguine. Mrs Ferrars resolved to speak to Mr Forgan as soon as she could find him alone. She contrived this later in the day, as she quartered the promenade, where he at last appeared, walking with some newly arrived visitors of the hospitable Mr King. These must needs be introduced to Mrs Ferrars, who placed herself in their way with a pertinacity worthy of her sister.

"I had hoped to see you," Lucy said after the introductions. "I have a message to give you." Taking the hint, the newcomers strolled on. Lucy added:

"It is not, I am afraid, to tell you that Louisa has relented."

"Relented? Miss Retford? No, I did not imagine that she would," said Mr Forgan, with a coldness in his voice that surprised and puzzled Lucy.

"I intend," she said, "that she may be brought to. I know you must be disappointed."

"It is a disappointment that I hope to survive. I must admit that I had formed, in some ways, a false estimation of Miss Retford. She is a charming young lady, but one whose decisions I would not query."

"She is stubborn, I agree, and sly, and fancies herself able to make decisions; but you should not be discouraged."

He smiled a little. "She, as you say, fancies what may not be always true. Some young ladies of that age are given to quirks of the imagination that verge upon the hysterical. She is not to blame for that, and the kindest method of dealing with her is to pay her no attention."

Lucy had never connected imagination nor hysteria with Louisa and did not dwell on the words, since more important to her was the recognition that Mr Forgan did not intend to persist in his proposal. It occurred to her, at the same moment, that if Mr Forgan were to be so kind as to pay Louisa no attention, it would severely affect the social life of their whole circle. She said, perturbed:

"I understand that you have told the Kings about what has passed between you and Louisa. Does this mean we shall lose your society altogether?"

At last, he himself looked awkward, but he said: "Of course, I shall hope to continue our engagements, with no embarrassment on any side. We had all arranged, had we not, to gather at the ball next week, and for the day after that, my sailing trip has been fixed. I must not disappoint my friends. I shall be equal to being in the same company as Miss Retford, should she also be equal to it."

"Oh, Louisa, is silent and mulish, and will pay no attention to anyone," Lucy declared, not pausing to consider that such a description would not recommend Louisa to Mr Forgan; although, for his ends, it did. He gave a smile more like his normal, and took leave with the civil hope of dancing with Mrs Ferrars at the ball.

Lucy was not dissatisfied with her reflections upon that interview. Mr Forgan was at any rate to meet Louisa again, and time might correct some strange notions he had of her: that she was – what had he said? – hysterical? Lucy was reminded that she must warn Nancy that Mr Forgan might not be as lost a cause as he seemed, lest Nancy try to take him up again as one of her beaux; although, from what Lucy had noticed at present, Nancy was showing much interest in that stern-faced curate who taught Latin, and attempting to lure him to the ball.

In this design Miss Steele had not yet succeeded. Only one Latin lesson intervened between the day of Mr Forgan's proposal and that of the ball, and at the Latin hour Miss Steele and her carpetwork were in attendance. In spite of Mr Dwyer's courteous regrets, and assertions that he had a prior engagement, Miss Steele continually interrupted the lesson with her invitations and protestations.

The lesson, in any case, did not go well. No one had disabused Mr Dwyer of the belief that Louisa was to marry Mr Forgan. Mr Dwyer did not understand why Louisa appeared so unhappy, or why she apologised so unhappily for the damage she had done to his book.

"But it is of no importance, I promise you," he said,

dismayed to see that tears spilled from her lowered eyes. He did not ask how the book had been smudged, but conjectured that Miss Retford had spilt water while filling a vase for flowers. "I only hope that you did not stain your gown with what must be inferior dye?"

Louisa could only shake her head.

"Many of my books have suffered in similar fashion by my own default. Only last week, I left my Bible out in the garden, and a shower of rain came on –"

"Lord," cried Miss Steele, "a clergyman who takes no care of his Bible should not be above a harmless pleasure like dancing."

Mr Dwyer bowed slightly in her direction before saying to Louisa: "Shall we begin, then, with the third chapter?"

Louisa nodded, and was about to open the book when she remembered that, again, she had run her fingers across her wet eyes. Mr Dwyer, noting her hesitation, opened the book for her and, as she did not start to read, did so himself.

"You have a good clear reading voice," remarked Miss Steele, not for the first time. "I declare, you will make me a faithful churchgoer if you try. I must come some time to hear you preach."

"Dr Mortimer does not often require that of his curates, ma'am."

"Then he is an old dog in the manger. Who would want to hear him, when there are better men to be had?"

Mr Dwyer responded to that merely by moving the book closer to his pupil and raising his good clear reading voice a little higher. Miss Steele decided that perhaps he was dull after all; one might suppose that he came here for nothing but to read his tiresome Latin, and that it would serve Louisa right if she were to end up by marrying such a man instead of the charming Mr Forgan.

12

Mr Forgan believed Louisa when she told him she had the pendant, and its disappearance was as perplexing to him as it was to her; nor had Signor Jacomo, when consulted, any theory to advance. The explanation, however, was this: Miss Steele, on one of her explorations of Louisa's possessions, came across the pendant in Louisa's jewel box. She said to herself: "This is pretty; I have not seen it before. Louisa will not mind if I borrow it, because she has never worn it." Pausing only to read a letter from Rowena Parr and to glance through Louisa's writing desk, Miss Steele went off to put the pendant in her own jewel box – or in one of them, for her collection of trinkets was extensive – and to forget for the present all about it.

It was not until she was deliberating over her accoutrements for the ball that she discovered the pendant again, and then she associated it not with Louisa, but with the crimson ribbons and sash of her gown. She had thought of wearing her gilt chain and locket, or her necklace of red glass beads; she now tried the pendant on the gilt chain, the chain together with the beads, the pendant on a silver ribbon, and every variation, even until the last moment before departure, when her sister was calling impatiently up the stairs for her. Miss Steele of a sudden perceived the solution that she had sought all day: the ring of the pendant was large enough for the bead necklace to pass through it. She threaded the pendant on to the necklace and fastened it, well pleased, round her throat.

No one noticed this splendour as they drove to the ball, but no one was in spirits for a ball; Mrs Ferrars declared herself ready to go back to London, as soon as tomorrow's sailing picnic was over, while Mr Costayne, the friend of Mr King's who had called for the ladies, remarked that the wind was rising and that the sea tomorrow would be unfit for sailing. Louisa was quiet as usual. "You might, Louisa," Mrs Ferrars urged her, "at the least smile, and try to make yourself agreeable. It is for your sake that I come to this evening's tedious event, and for the children's that I must go on the sea picnic tomorrow. I grow tired of wearing myself out to please others."

"George, I am sure, will be pleased to go sailing," Louisa said, a smile touching her face at the prospect.

"Oh, George I expect will fall overboard and drown, and then Robert and his mother will lay all the blame on me. See, we are arrived – Nancy, you are jabbing your fan into my arm –"

"Well, you are crushing my gown. Take care with your foot –"

They all emerged from the carriage in fair order, and entered the building. On the threshold of the ballroom, the first person they encountered was Signor Jacomo, and the first object upon which Signor Jacomo's gaze lit was Miss Steele's pendant.

His swiftness and presence of mind were commendable. "Miss Steele," he exclaimed, bowing, "how ravishing you look! Each time I see you, you are more tastefully adorned. May a humble foreigner be allowed the honour of kissing your hand?" In order to achieve this he seized the hand, turning so that Miss Steele perforce turned too, and was drawn aside from the doorway and into the screen of a palm tree in the corridor, unresisting, affecting laughter at his compliments. He continued:

"I must confess to you that, although in the course of my profession I have moved in the highest circles of England's society, I have seen no lady who dressed with more true elegance than you. You must forgive me if my admiration leads me into impertinence – But, the colour of your gown! The ornaments in your hair! All delights me. But, wait; one should not improve upon perfection. I feel – with deference – that your slender throat would appear more graceful with only its necklace; the addition of the other jewel destroys the line – Permit me –" Deftly, he stepped behind her, unfastened the necklace and slipped the pendant free of it. Replacing the necklace he faced her again, tilting his head as a connoisseur studies a work of art, meanwhile unobtrusively pocketing the pendant. "Ye-es; I believe I am right," he said after his scrutiny. "The line of the throat, broken only by the necklace, is ... swanlike. Your gracefulness is emphasised."

His seriousness had as great an effect as his praise on Miss Steele. Compliments she took as her due, even had she to invite them; but this earnest analysis of her beauty was new to her. Swanlike and elegant she posed herself before him, laughing but a little bashful. "La! sir, I have not been compared to a swan before. You flatter me too much." In her elation she had, as Signor Jacomo had hoped, forgotten about the pendant. He bowed and proceeded:

"No one could do that, I assure you. Now, although I know many partners are awaiting you, I am once again going to play the impertinent foreigner, and cut in upon them all by asking you for the honour of the first dance."

She could not refuse, nor would she have, had she been already engaged for the first dance. Advancing into the ballroom she was convinced that she outshone all the other ladies, and valued the conviction no less because it had come from little Mr Yakko – who, when one stood beside him in the set, appeared taller than one had remembered; and whose manner was fully attentive; her every word seemed to delight him.

It was true that Luigi Jacomo, moving among the ladies of upper English society, at concerts or as his pupils, had never met a lady who dressed as Miss Steele did, or one as amusingly stupid. He found her indeed delightful, in her assumption of gentility and in her lapses from it, and refreshing in her spontaneity. He set himself to divert her entirely from the recollection of that pendant and did not suppose he could be unsuccessful. He danced with her as often as decorum would permit, and interveningly, pressed any other gentleman at liberty to be presented to her. Miss Steele was passing a triumphant evening.

As Signor Jacomo led her to supper she paused to say to Louisa who sat by the wall: "Louisa, have you no partner? It is your own fault if you have not, because Mr Dwyer would surely have come had you persuaded him, but you must learn to attract the gentlemen for yourself. I cannot always be helping you."

It was not Louisa's want of partners this evening that grieved her, but a sense of isolation that arose not from her own solitude but from around her. Miss King, dancing with Mr Forgan, had smiled at Louisa but the smile had lingered in a stare of open curiosity; a little later, Louisa had noticed Miss King talking to Mrs Costayne, who then turned her eyes in Louisa's direction but averted them as their glances met. Mr Costayne then came and asked Louisa to dance, but as they did so he barely spoke, and bore himself towards her with a solemn sort of kindness; after the dance he seemed to enter into a private confabulation with his wife and Miss King, their heads together.

Louisa was not to know that Mr Forgan, as soon as Signor Jacomo had whispered to him that the pendant was retrieved, had begun to lay the foundation of a defence against any possible further trouble from Louisa: he hinted, with sorrow and sympathy, to his friends, that poor Miss Retford had spent so much time in study and reading that he was afraid her nerves were affected, and perhaps even her mind impaired.

Mrs Ferrars, yawning, called: "Louisa, come; if you and I must be neglected, you must serve my supper to me. Tell the servant I do not care for lobster ..." She led the way into the supper-room, where the laughter and clatter rang convivially. They found places at the end of a table by the door. "See," said Mrs Ferrars pointing with her fan, "Nancy is in fine fettle with herself. I wonder what that little organ-grinder can be saying to her."

Signor Jacomo was at that moment saying: "I envy you, Miss Steele, that your life is a succession of gaieties like this."

"La, I do not spend all my time at balls. You yourself seem to turn up at a good many."

"Recently, yes. But this summer has been a period of comparative leisure for me, that must end. I have my living to earn."

"And so shall – that is, the summer will end for all of us."

"And then you will leave Brightsea? Will you go to London with your sister?"

"I dare say. I have not decided. What affair is that of yours?"

"I implied only, that I shall be desolated to lose your company. I may be in London for part of the winter, and should be happy to think we might meet there, even should I soon leave Brightsea –"

"Soon leave? Why? And to go where?"

"Like you, I have not decided. Before long, I must spend some time at home. By 'home', I mean at my house in Milan, which is the nearest I have to a permanent abode. I am not so fortunate as you, in having a family to whom I may attach myself."

"Lord, if you mean Lucy, I do not wish to attach myself there. We have been like two cats in a bag of late. Where is Milan?"

"It is in Italy, dear lady; it is a great centre of the arts, and a thriving city. Have you not been there?"

"Abroad?"

"Perhaps you do not care for travelling?"

"I never had – no, I perhaps do not. What is your house like?"

"Oh, modest; very modest. It is no *palazzo*, but has a fine outlook and a walled garden whose variety of flowers would astonish you. I would very much like you to see it."

"How many bedrooms has it?"

"My dear Miss Steele, you cannot imagine I am suggesting any sort of impropriety?"

Miss Steele laughed heartily. "You cannot imagine either that I would consent to any. Does the house stand empty while you are away?"

"My man Guiseppe, and his wife, take care of it for me. Let me fill your glass ... And I have an enchanting white cat, named Filippo. I should very much," he added in a pensive tone, "like to observe the effect on you of Milan." He pondered this for a moment before adding: "However, such a scheme will have to remain a daydream."

Miss Steele, deprived of a daydream, felt more cheated than she would if deprived of an actuality. "I do not see why. I am as like as anyone, to travel to Italian cities with flowers and white cats. I am no old maiden aunt, not to be considered fit –"

"Dear Miss Steele, do not paint such a hideous picture of yourself, even in fun. It hurts me that you joke at your own expense. All the fine cities of the world, and its cats of every colour, I would willingly reveal to you, but I could not bear to submit you to scandal, nor could you bear to abandon your native country and language – Though, would you not be a little diverted to hear yourself addressed as 'Signora'?"

"Who is she?"

"That, dear lady, is the Italian title of a married woman."

"I see. Married? You are married?"

"Unhappily, not yet. My Signora also remains a daydream."

Miss Steele emptied her wineglass and sighed. "I have heard enough of daydreams. When does the dancing begin again?"

"At any moment. I am completely yours to command, signorina."

"Let us go, then," commanded Miss Steele, rising from the table in a flurry of flounces, surprised to discover that the sense of a daydream still accompanied her, rendering the lights of the room rosy, and her feet a little unsteady under her. "I have never enjoyed a ball so much," she told Signor Jacomo. "I shall think carefully over all you have said, when the dancing is finished, but I do not want to lose a moment of it. Signora," she added, pronouncing the word in imitation of him. "Is that what you said?"

"*Si* – Yes, signora; you speak good Italian."

They had re-entered the ballroom, where the vigour of the dancing throng made the floor vibrate under their feet. "I hope this floor is strong," remarked Miss Steele, whose own lingering unsteadiness increased the vibration. "It rocks under me. And that reminds me: Mr Costayne says the wind is rising. I hope it will not be rough on the sea when we go for our picnic tomorrow."

"Should the waves be dangerous," declared Signor Jacomo, "I would summon a dolphin and bear you shorewards on its back."

"Sir, you are too gallant," Miss Steele demurred.

Signor Jacomo was beginning to think so. He had enjoyed pouring out upon Miss Steele compliments and flatteries that no one else would have accepted without suspicion, but he must not risk her suspicion, nor any suspicion of the rest of the company that he was paying Miss Steele singular attention. Mercifully the ball was nearing its close, and it was on the advice of Mrs King and Mrs Ferrars that their party left before the end; Mrs King wanted everyone to be fresh for the start of the excursion tomorrow, and Mrs Ferrars could restrain her yawns no longer. Signor Jacomo and Miss Steele left the ballroom equally satisfied: he with the pendant in his pocket, and she with an unexpected new conquest to her credit. She received no praise for it from either her sister or Louisa, who for their separate reasons were indifferent to her success, so she could look forward only to a resumption of Signor Jacomo's admiration during tomorrow's voyage.

Signor Jacomo had anticipated this, and next morning found himself obliged to write several important letters, which unfortunately would constrain him to stay at the house. It began to seem, however, as if the sailing picnic would not in any case be feasible; the wind had, as Mr Costayne foresaw, risen, and although the sun shone, brisk waves slapped against the harbour wall where the party assembled. Only Miss Steele looked about for Signor Jacomo; everyone else gazed at the sky and the water.

"There are clouds massing," said Mr Costayne pointing westwards.

"But the sea is not too rough for us," Miss King protested.

"It will grow rougher, and we shall all be splashed with the spray," said Mrs Ferrars. "It will be cold, also, out on the water."

"Oh, ma'am," cried George, "we shall not mind a little breeze!"

"Be quiet, George."

Louisa said to him aside: "Do you not suppose Augusta will be afraid on the rough sea?"

"No, I shall hold her quite safe," he asserted.

Mr Forgan meanwhile was consulting the apt authority: the owner of the boat, and their navigator. Joseph Henson was a fisherman who had painted up his second boat, and provided awnings, for the carrying of pleasure parties. He stood now like everyone studying the weather, while his two sons who formed his crew waited, sitting on bollards and looking sceptical.

"Aye," said Joseph Henson at last, "it do look to turn dirty."

His sons nodded agreement, while the visitors called queries and objections. Joseph Henson hated to disappoint them, as well as to lose a day's hire; but he was an honest man and knew that the *Mary Belinda*, trim as she was under her layers of gay paint, was held together by little else and might not stand the battering of open sea if the weather worsened. Finally, seeing the pretty young lady and the little boy especially downcast, he offered a compromise:

"I tell you what I will do. No going out beyond the point and landing on the island, not today. That would mean facing her into deep sea just at tide turn. But how would you like to sail round in the bay in the lee of the cliffs, for a couple of hours? Better than nothing?"

The party consented to this and the embarkation began, with some commotion, as Mrs King sent her husband back to the carriage for extra shawls, and as it was decided that the picnic need not be carried but could be consumed on their return, so that must be taken back to the carriage, and as Miss Steele insisted that they should wait for Signor Jacomo who surely might still arrive; but eventually she was persuaded on board, and the patient Henson sons cast off their ropes; with Mr Henson at the wheel, the *Mary Belinda* slid out of the harbour and spread her sails to the breeze.

The delight of the majority of the voyagers was evident. Miss King exclaimed at the dark blue of the deeper water and the widening backward views of the town; Mrs Costayne cried out at the beauty of the diamonds of spray that leapt up to the boat's sides; Augusta in the bows, securely held by George's arms, screamed that she had seen a mermaid; Mr Costayne drew Mr Forgan's notice to the sea birds, asking their names; Louisa, leaning on the rail, gazed down into the waves in an interval of calm abstraction. While the sun shone, all was happiness. As Mr Costayne's clouds approached, and the colours of sea and sky faded, a growing chill was felt, and the size of the waves increased. Joseph Henson decided to turn back, and sent one of his sons to warn the little boy to hold his sister very tight. Broadside on to the waves, the *Mary Belinda* had need of all her layers of paint; the sails creaked and the wind whistled, Miss Steele shrieked with terror and Augusta and George shrieked with excitement. Louisa, still gazing down, saw such a chasm between the side of the boat and a wall of black water that she involuntarily clutched for a nearby rope of the rigging, which her groping hand missed; someone else's hand seized her shoulder and pulled her back from the sloping rail. She looked gratefully round, to see that the hand had been that of Mr Forgan. He had happened to be close behind her, talking to Mrs King, and his gesture had been as involuntary as Louisa's. She was dismayed that, in answer to her smile of thanks, he gave her only a cold unrecognising stare. He turned away from her at once and bent to murmur something to Mrs King, who cried:

"But she cannot have meant to throw herself –" before clapping her hand over her mouth. Mr Forgan bent to her again to whisper, but at that moment a wave tossed into the air a mass of spray that crashed with the noise of gunshot upon the awning above them. Mrs Ferrars remarked, in annoyance rather than in alarm:

"I knew this day was not fit for sea going."

"Soon be ashore again," bellowed Joseph Henson to them above the sounds of what seemed to the passengers a considerable storm. And indeed, his sons were already taking in sail, and the cliffs and houses drawing closer. There was surf at the base of the cliffs, but under the boat the waves were smoother. George could be heard deploring the brevity of their voyage, and Miss Steele deploring the spatter of spray on her gown and bonnet, as the *Mary Belinda* glided back into harbour.

Brief as their excursion had seemed to George, it was already well past midday. No one could decide on what to do next. They were to have had their picnic on the little beach below the harbour wall, but Mrs Ferrars pronounced that it was too cold.

"No, the sun is coming through again! It will be warm enough, below the wall, for us to sit," Miss King insisted.

"But we are wet," complained Mrs Costayne. "It will not be comfortable." She looked with disapproval at the bedraggled George and Augusta.

"I dare say," her husband mentioned, "the children are hungry."

Discussion became general and slightly acrimonious.

"It would be warmer to have our meal in the carriage."

"If we sit in the carriage we may as well go home in it."

"One does not take a picnic home; that defeats the purpose."

"Well, then what *is* our purpose?"

Mr Forgan, who was after all their host, was looked to for a solution, and he gave the verdict that, sheltered by the wall, they could enjoy their picnic in tolerable comfort. The servants were sent to bring the baskets from the carriage and, Miss King leaping ahead, his guests descended to seat themselves on the shingle. It may have been that Mr Forgan wished only to have the whole event over as soon as possible; on this day he had hoped to achieve success and wealth among the winding paths of the romantic island, whereas, now, he regarded the object of his quest merely with aversion. After directing the laying out of the picnic, he seated himself far from Louisa and responded only with a gloomy half-smile to the cheerfulness of Miss King.

Not only the children ate with almost indecorous speed. The creeping wind sought their shelter, the shingle did not form a soft couch, and grains of sand mingled with the food. The gathering had no unity; Mr and Mrs King entered on some domestic debate, Mrs Ferrars, aloof, was ostentatiously shivering, Miss Steele turning continually to see whether Signor Jacomo might not appear on the wall-top. Presently Louisa rose and followed the children, who, replete, were searching for shells at the water's edge; Augusta wished to make a necklace, this time for Molly. It was not long before the servants were summoned to pack up the repast.

"Now," called Mrs King in thankful release, "who is to come back in the carriage? Mrs Ferrars, shall we take you?

Or the children, if they are tired?"

"Do not wait for me; I shall walk," offered Miss King, with a glance of appeal at Mr Forgan, who accepted the offer:

"I shall see Miss King home."

"I thank you, but I am in no hurry," Mrs Ferrars replied to Mrs King. In truth she was anxious to be home and warm but, with carriages of her own in London, she chose to interpret Mrs King's tone as one of condescension. She called her children, scolding Augusta for being wetter than ever and for ruining her boots, while Miss King and Mr Forgan moved off and Miss Steele stood waiting to be invited to the carriage. Mrs King, however, assumed that the family from Stanley Crescent would not wish to be divided, and herself moved off in talk with Mrs Costayne.

"So we are to go on foot," lamented Miss Steele. "Well, I shall not care. The exercise will warm me, after that terrible boat, as well as that picnic – There was no salt in the meat, I declare. Besides, if I walk, I may meet some friends."

"And a fine spectacle you will make for your friends, with your bonnet all a tangle of sea spray, and sand on your gown."

Miss Steele had not thought of that. "Lord, I do think Mrs King could have taken me in the carriage. Why did you refuse her? Nor need you mock at me, Lucy. Your own face is bright red with the wind."

The sisters exchanged similar civilities until Mrs Ferrars, tiring, said: "I am going. You do as you wish; display your bonnet with its barnacles to Signor Jacomo and the rest of your beaux. Come, Louisa – I must take Augusta home directly, or she will cough all night. Where is George?"

Louisa coming towards the others paused to look about. "He was here, beside you, a moment ago. Has he gone up to the harbour?"

Augusta piped: "No, he ran off that way." She pointed to the base of the cliff at the other side of the small bay.

"Where has he gone? How tiresome he is, when he knows

we are going home. Louisa, go and find him."

Louisa about to obey paused again; George must have climbed over the rocks at the foot of the cliff, where the waves were swirling and receding. "I hope he is not gone far. I believe the tide is coming in."

"Of course he is not far away. He has been gone only five minutes and can have no reason for exploring in that direction."

"I am afraid he may have. He may have gone to look for the smugglers' caves he was so curious about."

"Caves? Well, you and Nancy can bring him back, and tell him he shall have a whipping for his caves." With that, Mrs Ferrars grasped her daughter's hand and departed.

Louisa asked Miss Steele: "Do you not think the tide is now at its height? How long should it take to turn? It could be dangerous, if George thought himself cut off, and tried perhaps to climb the cliff."

"Gracious, what do I know of tides? I am no fisherman. You had better call on that man who steered our boat for his help."

"I do not know where to find him, and it would take so long. I feel we should follow after George, to be sure he comes to no harm."

"Well, and how do you propose doing that? Would you have me go over those rocks, dragging my gown on them and tearing it? George will look out for himself. Boys are good at climbing; better than us."

"I shall go, then," decided Louisa. "Will you please tell Mrs Ferrars that I am seeking him?"

"Lord, you will overtake me before I am home," Miss Steele assured her, tweaking at her own damp bonnet ribbons.

Louisa stepped without difficulty over the rocks at the base of the cliff, to find herself in another small bay. It contained neither George nor, as far as she could discern, any cave in its crevice. At the further side of the bay a further ridge of vertical rock must lead to a next bay. On

Louisa went, clinging close to the cliff foot, for the sea seemed to be breaking here more violently, and spray drenched her before she was round the corner. Here was a repetition: a small bay, no little boy and no cave, and again, a sharp edge of cliff to be circumvented. Louisa could not tell how long all this was taking her, nor what state the tide was in, but certainly the sea was wilder and the wind cold. She leapt over her ankles in foam, slipping on wave-sucked pebbles, to arrive in the third bay; and here, to her relief, was George. He did not at first see her, because he was trying as she had feared to climb out up the cliff. She called as loud as she could, above the noise of wind and sea, and at last he looked down from the narrow greasy ledge from which he had been searching for an ascent. His face brightened with both reassurance and tears as he saw Louisa and she signed to him to climb down; this appeared more difficult than climbing up, but after some guidance from below he tumbled down the last ledge and embraced her.

"I was climbing up. I thought the tide was coming in and I could not go back. But you came by my way?"

"I did, and we must hurry back, because perhaps you are right about the tide." He was; since Louisa had reached the cove, the sea had gained, and now the waves hurled themselves at full height against the ridge of cliff behind them.

"Can we not climb up, Louisa?"

"No, George; look, the rock is wet and slippery, and probably much of it loose. You were lucky not to fall, as it was."

"Then what shall we do?"

"We shall have to wait until the tide drops a little way and we can go back. Let us sit on the ledge of rock above us. That should be clear of the full tide."

"Louisa, there is a cave. I was about to go in, but I saw the sea and was frightened. Shall we wait in the cave? It would be sheltered."

"But, George, did Mr Forgan not say that the caves were under water at high tide? I had rather we found a firm ledge, as high as we can, and settled there to watch. You must wrap my cloak round you. It is wet, but thicker than your own coat. First, we must reach a safe height." They helped each other on to a wide shelf of rock above the entrance to George's cave. George insisted that Louisa's cloak be wrapped round both of them.

"– Because is it not cold, Louisa, for a summer day? I suppose it is nearly evening. What will my mother say? We shall be late home. Will she not wonder where we are?"

"I told her – that is, I told Miss Steele where I was coming, and they will guess that we are together."

"When you do not come back either, they will come to find us, surely."

"They will not need to; soon, we shall find our own way back."

After an interval George asked: "How soon, Louisa?"

"As soon as the water is low enough."

"Yes. I was wondering, you see," he said in a diffident tone, "how long that will be."

So was Louisa. As they watched, a very high wave swept up the beach below them and poured into the mouth of the cave. Surf swung across the bay, filling it with white foam. George remarked:

"You see, if they came in a boat, they could not reach us. Any more than the excise officers could reach the smugglers."

"We shall have to pretend that we are smugglers, George."

"Oh, yes. Let us be smugglers. Your cloak is so thick, Louisa that it keeps both of us warm, does it not?" he added, his teeth chattering.

Louisa made an effort to control her own shudders of cold. "Yes, we keep one another warm when we sit close like this." The foam in the bay beneath them was flushed with pink, reflected from the setting sun. Louisa wondered without daring to speak it: if it grows dark before the tide drops, how are we to find our way down from this ledge and back to the harbour?

13

Mrs Ferrars hurried home, delivered Augusta to Jenny for liniment and linctus, then applied herself to the relief of her own discomforts. Her face was not bright red, as Nancy had unkindly told her, but Lucy's complexion and hair had suffered from the sea spray and wind; she did not hear her sister come in, nor wonder about the movements of anyone else; it was some while later that Jenny came to her door to say that it was past Master George's bedtime, and could he please come?

"He is not with me, Jenny. Ask Miss Retford."

"I think she is not back yet, ma'am."

Miss Steele was inquired of. "Are they not home?" she said. "Well, Louisa is taking care of George. She bade me tell you so. They will not be far off."

Lucy now observed that the clouded day had darkened early, and began to be anxious. When she heard that Louisa and George had been left on the beach, she blamed Miss Steele for her negligence. "You should have waited for them, Nancy – or told me at once. They were round the rocks? They will have been cut off by the tide –"

"I am sure it was not my fault. I told Louisa not to go climbing and spoiling her dress. And the tide will be falling by now –"

It may have been, but Lucy had no leisure for calculating

it, nor for entering into recriminations with her sister. She told John to run as fast as he could down to the harbour, and call out helpers to search for George and Louisa. By the time Lucy was dressed and had followed him, a group of men was already gathered with lanterns on the little beach of today's picnic. "They must be in one of the coves," Joseph Henson told her. "No one has seen them. We shall soon find them and bring them safe back. Do not worry."

He led the way round the cliff foot, which was by now exposed to the level of the late afternoon's tide again. Lucy could not but worry, as she waited at the water's edge, reckless of the wind and spray now. It seemed for hours that she stood there, staring at the unyielding cliff, paying no heed to the women from the village who had arrived for her support or from curiosity. When, at last, a ray of lantern light shone from behind the cliff, and shadowed figures appeared, moving slowly as if burdened, one of the women had to restrain her from running on to the rocks to meet them.

"Let them down, you will but hinder them –"

The men's boots crashed on the shingle. Joseph Henson shouted: "They are alive but must be sheltered quick. We shall take them to my house –"

"Nay, William has his cart here," shouted back someone else. "Take them straight home, among the straw."

Lucy had shaken off the woman's hand and dashed forward. In the light of a lantern George's face was white and shrunken, but as she called his name he opened his eyes and said:

"I am sorry, ma'am."

George was barely conscious, but a part of his mind perceived and marvelled at the expression of terror with which his mother looked down at him. He had not known that anything could ever frighten her. Perhaps he himself, after this, would never be so frightened of her again.

George, swaddled in the warm straw of the cart, was beginning to recover by the time he was back at Stanley

Crescent. His mother and Jenny attended to him and put him to bed, while Miss Steele was urged to see to Louisa whom John carried upstairs still insensible.

"I shall not know what to do to her," cried Miss Steele, thrown into a frantic alarm by the sight of Louisa's blue-tinged face.

"It is you who claims to be in charge of her," retorted Mrs Ferrars from above. Fortunately, Molly had come upstairs, and after looking at Louisa said:

"John, go for a doctor. Miss Steele, help me undress her."

Louisa and George had, as she had feared, been overtaken by twilight before the tide receded. They had been overtaken too by such cramps and chills that, when the lanterns of their rescuers appeared below, they could not climb down; Louisa was already on the verge of faintness. It was not until the small hours of next morning that she began to come to herself, and then it was into a delirium of dark ocean waves.

She heard a distant voice saying: "Do you think she will die?"

Another answered: "The doctor said we must hope, Miss Steele."

The doctor had indeed admitted Louisa's feverish chill to be assuming a very grave nature, and had promised to visit her again in the morning. Molly and Jenny sat with her, folding cold cloths to her brow, while Mrs Ferrars sat with the now slumbering George, and Miss Steele retired to bed, overcome, she announced, by this tragedy.

Louisa, sunk again in her nightmares, accepted that she was about to die. Almost, to escape from these dark waves and from her previous perplexities, she might have been glad to. Yet, a twinge of memory stirred her: what was it that she had neglected to do? Before she died, she must ... She could not remember. She opened her eyes, and saw daylight, but did not immediately know where she was. The window, instead of blue with Brightsea sky, was grey as winter, and a fire burnt in the grate, beside which stood someone whom Louisa could not identify. Then memory stirred again:

"Mrs Benson," said Louisa in weak astonishment.

Mrs Benson hurried to the bed, pleased by this sign of recovery, and started to smooth the pillows and lay her hand on Louisa's brow. "Yes, it is Mrs Benson, my dear, and I am going to take care of you, and you will soon be well again."

Early this morning Mrs Benson, who had been among the watchers on the beach, had come to Stanley Crescent to inquire after Miss Retford, and had arrived while the doctor was there. He had been about to send for a nurse, and had been glad of the opportune advent of Mrs Benson, whom he knew and trusted. So here Mrs Benson was, preparing a soothing draught and murmuring soothing words.

Louisa might have taken Mrs Benson for a harbinger of death, and felt herself about to be designated 'poor' Miss Retford; but her mind's confusion yielded a part of what she had been striving to remember:

"Oh, Mrs Benson, the pendant is gone again, and I do not know who has it."

"Hush, now, do not trouble yourself about anything. You must rest. Let me raise your head, so that you can take this draught. It will help you to sleep."

Sleep Louisa did, but fitfully, tossing, compelling herself to rouse yet speaking now and then out of her dreams. "I must tell her," she said. "I should have told her." And later: "Mrs Benson!"

"What is it, my dear?"

"You must not let Mr Forgan into your house again."

"No, no, we have agreed that I shall not. Rest yourself."

"And you must warn Miss King, for no one will believe me. She would not believe me. Yet I should have tried to warn her. I must see Miss King directly. Would she come before it is too late?"

Towards evening Louisa's fever heightened, and Mrs

Benson, fearing that Louisa's agitation subscribed to that, went to Mrs Ferrars to say:

"Beg pardon, ma'am, but has Miss Retford a friend of the name of Miss King? She very much desires a Miss King to come to her."

"Isabella King? No, I am sure Louisa is not at all fit for visitors, and that King girl would chatter her head off and do Louisa harm."

"It does her harm, I think, to fret as she does. She is not at all well again. Her mind is much troubled."

"I had better come myself to see her," said Lucy, who in her fatigue after the terror of George's danger had been glad to leave Louisa to the care of nurse and servants. The care of Miss Steele, still in terror lest Louisa die while in her charge, was negligible; now she too came up to Louisa's room, following Lucy and peeping over her shoulder at the bed where Louisa, flushed and agitated, was struggling to rise. Mrs Benson persuaded her to lie down, but Louisa was crying:

"I must see Miss King. Someone must believe me. I cannot find the pendant. I must search for it again. I must tell her of Mr Forgan's wickedness, although he has told her that I am not to be believed. I must tell Mr Forgan to go away, because he knows himself that he is a thief. I cannot tell what to do –"

Lucy was disturbed by this raving; she remembered that Mr Forgan had described Louisa as hysterical, and it seemed he was right. She said in a firm tone:

"Louisa, calm yourself. This is all nonsense about pendants and thieves. It is the fantasy of fever, and you will make yourself more ill with it."

"She will, poor lamb," murmured Mrs Benson smoothing the pillows. Louisa turned her face into the pillows, weeping:

"He is cruel and a thief and I alone know of it ..."

"If that is what her fantasy tells her of him," remarked Lucy, "it is no wonder she refuses to marry him."

"*She* marry *him*? I should say not," exclaimed Mrs Benson.

Two factors at this moment operated against Louisa's being believed: Miss Steele, it need not be said, had forgotten all about any pendant so did not contribute any credence to Louisa's tale; and Lucy, tired and anxious, was irritated by Mrs Benson's comment. She said:

"What you should say, nurse, is beyond your duty. Please see that Miss Retford is comfortable, and give her a draught to calm her." She left the room, disdaining to discuss Louisa's private affairs with a mere servant; while Miss Steele, following her sister on tiptoe, had no idea that she had seen Mrs Benson before in her life.

"Lord, Lucy," Miss Steele complained on the stairs, "if she should die, how am I to tell her grandfather? You must write the letter for me."

"Certainly I shall not," declared Lucy, adding no reassurance. She was as irritated by Nancy's ineffectual panic as by the nurse's interference. Whereupon Miss Steele, her optimism broken, burst into tears and sat at the table to begin the composition of her letter, ruining many sheets of paper to no effect.

During that night Louisa's fever, however, subsided a little. The next morning she fell into a exhausted sleep that Mrs Benson hoped would prove refreshing. It was the morning for a Latin lesson and Mr Dwyer rang the doorbell at his appointed time. He was surprised by John's surprise at seeing him.

"But, sir, there can be no lesson today. Miss Retford is very ill."

"What is the matter?" asked Mr Dwyer in alarm. John began to explain, but meanwhile George, much restored but commanded to remain resting in the back parlour, had put his head out of it to see who had come to the door; convalescence bored him, and he was delighted to see Mr Dwyer as a distraction. He came running down the hallway crying:

"Mr Dwyer, we are all in such distress. I went to look for the caves, and it was the wrong time of the tide, as well as naughty of me to run off, and Louisa came to find me and we sat on the cliff and pretended to be smugglers and you could not imagine how rough the sea was, and how cold we were, but we were rescued, but now Louisa is so ill, a nurse has come, and the doctor again, and they will not let anyone see her. Oh, sir, what if Louisa should die?"

Jenny, in pursuit of George, now approached to say: "You must not think of that, Master George. Mrs Benson has told me Miss Retford is better this morning." Her comfort was as welcome to Mr Dwyer as to George. She led George away, against his demands that he have a Latin lesson to himself; for which Mr Dwyer was thankful, since he hardly felt fit to teach. He returned home to waste the day in trying to read or write or talk to his sister, who, concerned for Miss Retford, became almost equally concerned for her brother. They sent to inquire in the evening, and heard that Miss Retford was still improving; when they sent next morning, the report was as encouraging. Miss Dwyer said:

"Martin, do you think I should be allowed to visit Miss Retford?"

His grateful look contradicted his words: "I do not suppose so."

"But I could make the attempt. They can only deny me. I shall promise not to disturb her. I could at the least tell you how she looks."

"Are you equal to such exertion?"

"You know I am. You can drive me to the door and wait, if you wish."

John did not immediately deny Miss Dwyer, who for all her gentleness of manner possessed a quiet authority. It happened that the ladies were shopping, so he summoned Mrs Benson, who formed the same estimate of Miss Dwyer, as an undisturbing visitor of the sick; which indeed Miss Dwyer was, from her practice in her brother's parish. Pausing only to ask whether Miss Dwyer were sure she was not Miss King, Mrs Benson led her upstairs.

Louisa today was mending in health, if not in spirits; she felt extremely weak and lonely, and the sweetness of Miss Dwyer's greeting brought her to tears. Miss Dwyer, seating herself beside the bed, at once asked, taking Louisa's hand in hers:

"My dear child, what is troubling you so?"

She was irresistible. After some incoherent words of deprecation and apology, Louisa found herself telling the whole story. From Miss Dwyer's sympathetic attentiveness she knew that she was believed, and the relief of this was so great that Louisa grew calm and even stronger. She ended:

"I do not know what I was saying when I was feverish, and naturally no one would believe me, when I have no longer the pendant –"

"I believe you," said Miss Dwyer, simply. "No, do not cry any more. I am sure you could scarcely believe it yourself, that this Mr Forgan should be so base. But you have no reason to fear him, nor need you meet him again. Put him out of your mind. As for warning Miss King, you may still do so, if you think it your duty, but I fancy it will be to little effect, if she admires him; ladies will admit to errors in their judgement, but not in their affections."

"I will be guided by anything you say. Oh, I so much wished to ask Mr Dwyer what I should do, but I dared not. Who can have taken away the pendant? You believe, that it was in jewel box?"

"Now, do not excite yourself again. I shall ask the nurse to come and bathe your tears away, and perhaps bring you a little broth. All will pass. You are not without friends, my dear."

This was evident, when Miss Dwyer called for Mrs Benson, who came bustling, to be told by Louisa: "Oh, Mrs Benson, I have repeated all of it to Miss Dwyer, and she believes me."

"Indeed, who would not, except the wicked man himself, who pretends not to, and some impatient ladies I had better not name."

"You too know Mr Forgan, do you?" asked Miss Dwyer, whereupon Mrs Benson abandoned her patient and stood arms akimbo while she regaled Miss Dwyer with the history of her own dealings with Mr Forgan.

This was confirmation, had Miss Dwyer needed it, but she was no nearer to imagining what help she could give; nor had she now the chance to speak, for meanwhile the ladies were returned from their shopping and Miss Steele, hearing that Louisa had a visitor, entered the room.

"Oh," she cried, "it is Miss Dwyer! How do you do, and how does your brother? You must give him my compliments. I have not seen him this long age, because we have been quite cut off from society with all the fuss over George and Louisa, but now that Louisa grows better, I hope we shall be out and about again. You look less thin; you are better too? You must bring your brother to the next ball, for he promised me to come to the last, and although I have since made *commitments* elsewhere, I shall contrive to spare him a dance."

Contriving not to commit her brother, Miss Dwyer took her leave, with an assurance to Louisa that she would visit her again. As Miss Steele accompanied her downstairs, Miss Dwyer thought to mention:

"Miss Retford has spoken to me of her refusal of Mr Forgan, and of the doubts she has of his character. I hope, as her duenna, you will be able to guard her from him in future?"

"I am no sort of a Jew-Anna, whoever that might be, and as for Mr Forgan, why, he is quite the gentleman and quite a special friend of mine, if not the most special, of course. If Louisa does not want to marry him, that is her own affair. John!" she hallooed down the hallway, "Here is Miss Dwyer going; do you expect me to open the door myself?"

Miss Dwyer, as her brother drove her home, informed him of all she had learnt, after undertaking that Miss

Retford's life was no longer in any danger. Mr Dwyer was both concerned and baffled; from the last he knew, Miss Retford was engaged to Mr Forgan, whom Mr Dwyer had scarcely met; the Dwyers' circle of friends nowhere intersected the Kings'. "Can the man be as perfidious as she says?" he wondered.

"You see; you doubt her too?"

"No. If you do not, certainly not." He added: "I have been at a loss all along to understand how Miss Retford comes to be among such people. She tells me she has a grandfather; what can he be about, to confide her to the care of a vulgar monster like Miss Steele?"

"Martin, that is not the voice of charity."

With a rueful smile Mr Dwyer admitted: "I have little charity where that lady is concerned, I am afraid. What makes me forget myself is, in fact, that I see nothing we can do to help. Do you require me to speak to Miss – King, was it? Or should I remonstrate with Mr Forgan himself? Either would be impertinent, and officious."

"And useless," added Miss Dwyer.

"Nevertheless, some gesture should be made," decided her brother with resignation rather than with enthusiasm. "I shall discover where he stays – it is at the house of the Kings, you said? – and I shall call upon him, merely to state that his dishonesty is known. I shall await no response from him. Merely, I wish him to understand that Miss Retford has sympathisers. If he is as suave a villain as I suppose, he will laugh at me; if he is an uneasy villain, he will threaten me with the law of slander. In either case, he and I will both wish to avoid a discussion. Our interview will be brief and, as you point out, useless."

However, as he must do what little he could, Mr Dwyer found out the address of the Kings' house and presented himself there early next day. Mr Forgan was at home, and the encounter between the two gentlemen was as brief and inconclusive as Mr Dwyer had foreseen. Mr Forgan fell into his first category, and heard his statement with a cool smile.

"My dear sir, if you choose to act upon the allegations of a hysterical young girl in a high fever, please take your protestations elsewhere. I thank you for your judgement of my merits, and must beg you to excuse me; I am engaged to walk out immediately."

Mr Dwyer bowed without further speech and withdrew, feeling his gesture wasted, his judgement of Mr Forgan's merits suspended.

14

The cold and grey week of Louisa's illness threatened the death of summer. Candles were lit in the evenings and no more parasols seen on the promenade. The thoughts of many turned inland, towards the hearths and convivialities of autumn. Lucy Ferrars resolved to return to London.

The shock of George's danger had been salutary to her. She felt she had neglected him, and other responsibilities besides; absence made her husband's weaknesses pitiable; she regretted that she had come to Brightsea on some pretext that now seemed frivolous. Had she wished to annoy Nancy, she had been well repaid by the annoyance Nancy had caused her; in comparison with that, the haughty petulance of the senior Mrs Ferrars might be restful. As Louisa was not to marry Mr Forgan, Lucy felt her own mission here unfulfilled, but she had lost interest in it, as well as in any renewal of the social gaieties to which Nancy so eagerly looked forward. Nancy's coy excitement over some new beau set Lucy's nerves increasingly on edge; Nancy would not reveal his name, and Lucy did not want to

know it. No one in Brightsea could be fit for anyone but
Nancy, who was welcome to her own winks and hints.
Nancy was welcome ever to Mr Forgan, whom Lucy now
distrusted, since it was he with his romances about
smugglers who had sent poor George into peril. It was time
for Lucy to take her children home, and to resume her own
pleasures there, as well as her duties.

Louisa was downstairs again, and the sun shone, if its
heat was less striking. Mr and Miss Dwyer came to take
Louisa for a drive in the country. "Oh well," observed Miss
Steele, "I do not much care that they did not invite me, for I
have much to see to. Besides, his sister is gone with him. I
expect they mean to be kind to Louisa."

They did; they meant to give her change of air and scene;
they did not speak of Mr Forgan, nor of Mr Dwyer's
interview with him.

Mr Dwyer might have been surprised to know that his
approach to Mr Forgan had had its effect. Mr Forgan was
not at all pleased that his previous life should be talked of,
even by an interfering cleric. As aware as anyone that the
summer must end, Mr Forgan had been considering his
future, and this depended in part upon the good opinion of
the Costaynes. They and he had not met until this season,
and he had made his usual excellent impression on them.
After leaving the Kings', the Costaynes proposed to take a
house in Bath for some weeks, and it would suit Mr Forgan
very well to receive an invitation there. The Costaynes were
evidently rich, and had spoken of nieces. The episode of
Louisa Retford had left an uneasy aftertaste; Mr Forgan
was for once a little apprehensive lest scandal overtake him,
lest he lose popularity. He hoped to be clear of Brightsea
unblemished, yet could not but feel that his eminence was
insecure. He questioned that he had been wise to malign
Miss Retford, however cautiously, since it appeared she
stood higher now in general opinion: from village to
servants to the houses of the town was spreading the tale of
the young lady who had so bravely gone to the rescue of a

little boy trapped by the tide, and who had made herself critically ill by the exploit.

Isabella King declared: "I should never have been so brave. Do you not remember how rough the waves were? Louisa is a heroine!"

Hoping that he would not need to outwit this heroine, Mr Forgan still determined to protect his position. He sought Signor Jacomo:

"Luigi, what have you done with that d – pendant? You had better dispose of it."

"I? But you have it yourself," returned Signor Jacomo across the top of the pianoforte.

"No, you forget: you told me you took it from Miss Steele –"

"You forget, rather, my dear James. I handed you the pendant in the passage of the supper room, at the end of the ball."

"I swear you did not."

"Swear away; I must practise this accompaniment."

"Where in the world, swearing apart, can it be?"

"Do not worry yourself; it will turn up."

"I am afraid it might do just that – inconveniently."

Mr Forgan searched in vain for the pendant, whose adventures might here be pursued: It had been given by Signor Jacomo at the ball to Mr Forgan who, so swiftly as perhaps to conceal the action from himself, wrapped it in a kerchief and dropped it into the skirt pocket of his evening coat. Next morning, before Mr Forgan was awake, the coat was duly taken by Mr King's manservant, along with the other garments from the ball, to the wardrobe. Mr Forgan could afford no manservant of his own but when visiting had to depend on the house servants such as Mr King's Arthur, who performed his duties for Mr Forgan in a somewhat perfunctory manner, since Mr Forgan was more lavish with his thanks than with his purse. When he came to the coat, Arthur drew from its pocket a kerchief that enwrapped a piece of jewellery. He laid the jewel on top of a linen press, threw the kerchief on to the washing heap, and set about sponging the coat. At that moment Mrs King's maid came into the wardrobe complaining, and tossed a stained pillow on to the linen press. The pillow skimmed across the press and knocked the pendant down behind, where it lodged between the wall and the press and where it remained; at least until after the end of this narrative. Arthur, finished with the coat, placed a clean kerchief in its pocket and, seeing nothing on the top of the press when the maid had removed the pillow, took the coat back with the rest of Mr Forgan's clothes.

Mr Forgan after fruitless search appealed again to Signor Jacomo, who became less solicitous than before as Mr Forgan displayed anxiety. The two friends were indeed about to suffer their first serious rift. Mr Forgan in his consternation was on the verge, too, of losing some of the confidence that had supported him throughout his life. He was on the verge also of the downhill slide that this can entail: anxious, he would begin to seek favour instead of commanding it, and his charm would become false as he exerted it for his own safety rather than for his pleasure in it. He was on the way to become a hanger-on and a petty schemer, desperate always for money and friends; it would require no action of the Marchendales' to achieve the destruction that Mr Forgan would bring upon himself.

As he wanted to rely more on his friend Luigi Jacomo he was forced to admit that Luigi was unreliable. He refused to believe that Luigi had not the pendant, and this suspiciousness, growing from Mr Forgan's unease, Signor Jacomo did not find amusing. His intuitions recognised the self-distrust behind Mr Forgan's distrust of him; weakness in James, Luigi Jacomo admitted, was disgusting. His only advice was: "You would do as well to flee before the thing does turn up."

Almost, Mr Forgan agreed, such was his bewilderment. He wanted to ask Luigi: whither? But Signor Jacomo would not pause in his strumming.

At about that same moment, Miss Steele in her room was planning her dress for the concert at the Spring Pavilion which was to be her first social sortie since the ball. She laid out her jewellery; she had chosen to wear her crimson sash and blue sprigged gown; when she held the red glass necklace against her swanlike throat, she was compelled to admit that, against this gown, the effect was too plain. She tried to remember what she had worn last time; Mr Yakko, or rather, Signor Yakko had thought her over-adorned; but, with what? All she could recollect was that she had worked herself into a fine frenzy until the last moment, with Lucy screaming for her and jewellery all over the dressing-table. Miss Steele knew something was missing ... Oh yes: the pendant with the garnets. Now she thought of it, it was Louisa's, and Miss Steele had borrowed it. But what had she done with it? Signor Jacomo's sleight of hand was obscured by the memory of his compliments and Miss Steele concluded that she must have replaced the pendant in Louisa's jewel box. Taking with her an amber pendant also borrowed from Louisa, which she might as well return since she did not herself much care for it, Miss Steele went to Louisa's room, knowing Louisa to be downstairs.

Miss Steele had been mistaken; Louisa was sitting by her window with a book, and raised her head surprised as Miss Steele burst into the room.

Surprised herself, Miss Steele said with a casual air: "Oh; Louisa. Here is your amber bauble I am bringing back, and I should like to borrow your pendant with the garnets, if that suits you."

Louisa laid down her book and came to stand gazing bemused at Miss Steele. "My pendant with the garnets?" she echoed. "Have you seen it?"

"Oh, yes, I borrowed it, you know, but I must have returned it, for it is not in my boxes. It will suit my sprigged gown. Where is it?"

"So it was you who took it? Miss Steele, can you remember when that was?"

"Lord, Louisa, I have no idea. What a fuss you make about a simple loan. Well, if you are going to be ungenerous about it, I will not make any fuss either."

"Miss Steele – please wait." Louisa in her eagerness laid her hand on Miss Steele's arm, and as Miss Steele could perceive that Louisa was in no way displeased, she conceded:

"Well, what is it?"

"I wish you could tell me whether you wore the pendant at anytime."

"I suppose so."

"You took it out of the house?" persisted Louisa, curious, and in truth comforted to know that it was only Miss Steele who had removed the pendant. Louisa reproached herself for not imagining this earlier, familiar as she was with Miss Steele's magpie attitude to all trinkets, her own or those of others. It was only because it had been that pendant in question that Louisa had imagined a theft more sinister, more occult, without at all explaining it.

"Well, I suppose I did," Miss Steele agreed. "I remember now, it was on the evening of the ball. I wore it with my crimson sash –"

"I do not remember that you wore a pendant at the ball?"

"No, as it happened I did not, because – I changed my mind."

"Then, where is the pendant now?"

"Good gracious, how should I know? It is for you to take care of your own possessions," said Miss Steele, treasuring her memory of Signor Jacomo's praise; but the memory must not remain entirely hidden, it was too precious for that; she added, regarding herself in Louisa's glass: "I do remember, that I took off the pendant before I began dancing, because a friend of mine told me that I appeared more elegant without it."

"What friend was that, Miss Steele?"

"La! Louisa, stop this teasing. You can wager you will

never get me to name a name."

"Was it Signor Jacomo?" asked Louisa in direct inquiry, which caused Miss Steele to put her hands over her face and break into coy titters, shake her head in protest, and hurry exclaiming from the room. In the doorway she turned back and dropped her hands to whisper:

"You will not give me away?"

"No, I will not," replied Louisa, at a loss about what it was she must not divulge, her mind occupied in the pursuit of the elusive pendant. So, if Signor Jacomo had advised Miss Steele to take it off, and it was no longer in Miss Steele's keeping, presumably it was Signor Jacomo who had kept it. Louisa could find no fault in this speculation, long as she considered it. The conclusion was, that the pendant had found its way by now back to Mr Forgan. Louisa's evidence was gone, but so was most of her perplexity. She earnestly hoped that Mr Forgan would make no further use of the pendant as a means of incrimination, but saw no way of preventing him. She must tell Mrs Benson of this development, however, and Miss Dwyer too; for, although Miss Dwyer and Mr Dwyer urged Louisa to think no more about Mr Forgan, they must be interested to hear the explanation of the pendant's vanishing.

The pendant, upon that, vanished from among Louisa's worries for the present. It was Miss Steele who, later, recollected: "When I think of it, Signor Yakko did not give me the pendant back. That was careless of him. I hope he has not lost it, because indeed it is Louisa's, and I am always very careful of other people's possessions." She fancied that Signor Jacomo, at tomorrow's concert, might replace the pendant as reverently as he had before removed it; he would allow that, with the sprigged gown, it added to her gracefulness; she dwelt on this fantasy for the rest of that day.

Engrossed in this and in re-arranging her costume for the concert, Miss Steele did not pause to ask herself what it was that kept Lucy so busy; later, when she met Jenny carrying upstairs an armful of clean linen, she was told that Mrs Ferrars was seeing to the packing of her boxes and the children's, ready for setting out to London. Miss Steele sought her sister in dismay.

"Lucy, you are not meaning to go away, and leave me here, with all the bills and household matters to see to!"

"You should have been seeing to them all along," Lucy reminded her. "You should be grateful that I have helped you. Mind that you see to the tidying of the house when you leave, as well, and submit all the accounts to the solicitors. See that the tradesmen do not charge too much, or the servants pilfer when you go; and there is the work to be done on the blocked drainpipe."

"Gracious, I cannot concern myself with drainpipes."

"For how long is the house taken?" went on Lucy unheeding.

"I do not know. What does it matter?"

"Not at all, except that you will need a roof over your head. From what I have understood, you must leave here at the end of September. Now listen to me, Nancy, I shall be very busy in London, with many friends to meet again, and Lord knows what in settling my own household matters. I do not want you arriving pretending you have nowhere to live, borrowing money and plaguing me. You must find someone to visit; you could go to the Palmers again, or to Delaford might be wiser; they have not had you so recently."

"Oh, I shall have no need to trouble them at Delaford," Miss Steele stated in a lofty voice. "I shall have a roof over my head, and it might astonish you to know where it is to be."

Lucy was not at leisure to be astonished; she continued in counting George's stockings, frowning over the poor order in which Jenny had kept them.

15

Miss Steele did not know whether to be disappointed or elated when she understood that she alone from Stanley Crescent was to attend the concert. Lucy ordained that Louisa was not yet strong enough to go out in the cooler evening air, and added that she herself was tired of the society of Brightsea.

"Ah, but you have formed no attachments among it!" said Miss Steele in a mysterious tone.

"My husband will be glad to know that."

Lucy and the children were to depart in the early morning of the day after the concert, a reason for social abstinence that Lucy did not enlarge upon. Miss Steele, who had settled with herself that she would receive Signor Jacomo's proposal during the concert's intermission, hoped only that she would wake in time to tell Lucy her amazing news (that Lucy would be amazed, Miss Steele could well foresee) – or might it be more effectively done by letter? No – to arrive in London, and present 'my husband' – that would be the amazement to eclipse all.

So, resigned to attending the concert alone, resolved not to become mixed up with anyone who would bar Signor Jacomo's access, Miss Steele relinquished her first scheme of amazing Lucy on the spot, and gave great care to her appearance. As jewellery, she finally decided on the red glass beads and her silver chain below them; at the last moment she added her locket to the chain, because, this evening, she must look at her most elegant.

The concert room was already half full, although she had arrived early. She chose a chair at the end of a line, and would not move from it when Miss King came up to ask her to join their party.

"You seem lonely here," Miss King explained.

"I shall not be lonely for long."

"Why, is Louisa coming? How is she? I so much want to see her, and to tell her how much I admire her bravery."

Louisa, brave? wondered Miss Steele, but she did not encourage Miss King in conversation. Glancing about her, she saw no one else likely to approach; Dr and Mrs Aylward came in, but passed her with a bow; their doctor son Miss Steele despaired of, for his delays seemed endless; but still they had rid themselves of the disagreeable Mrs Mitchin, and in any case, the Aylwards could not be of importance to Miss Steele now. It was a relief that Mrs Yarrow had evidently despaired of her own son, and let him back to his law studies and herself back to her home, whose whereabouts Miss Steele had forgotten. At one moment Miss Steele almost despaired of Signor Jacomo's coming this evening; the Kings and their party were all gathered, at the top of the room. However, for anything musical, he surely must come; and so he did, placing himself not with Mr King's group but alone, as if he wished to hear the singer from close by; but Miss Steele knew that he wished, rather, to demonstrate that he, like Miss Steele, was at present unattached.

The singer on this occasion was an operatic baritone, whose growlings Miss Steel found hideous; she strove however, to appear as absorbed in the music as, from her sidelong scrutiny, she guessed Signor Jacomo to be. At the intermission he rose, applauding and beaming, but then walked out into the corridor. Miss Steele stared after him horrified, before she recollected that she had a pretext for making an approach to him herself. She smoothed her gown and hastened out of the room in pursuit, pushing against the stream of people making for the supper tables. Outside, she soon saw Signor Jacomo, talking to the man who had accompanied the singer on a pianoforte. Miss Steele, tapping Signor Jacomo's shoulder with her fan, interrupted them:

"Signor Yakko, good evening to you. I have something to ask you." He bowed, in greeting to her and in apology to the accompanist, and let himself be drawn aside.

"Have you the pendant? I must take it to Louisa. I forgot to tell you that it is hers."

"A pendant, dear lady?"

"You must remember. At the ball, you took it from my throat, because you said I was over-elegant."

"Ah, *si* – that small piece of jewellery. No, I regret, it is not in my possession."

"Lord. Have you lost it? I had but borrowed it, from Louisa."

"I surmised as much. No, I myself have not lost it. Why do you not ask Mr Forgan about it?"

"Why should I? It has nothing to do with him. For that matter, why do you not ask him for me?"

"Ah, no," said Signor Jacomo in a persuasive tone, "the question would come better from you. You will find him at supper; will you not ask him – to please me?" The glint of his eye Miss Steele took as conspiratorial sympathy. She replied archly:

"To please you, sir, I would do anything." She crossed the concert room; beyond, where the tables were set out, she soon descried Mr Forgan, whose tall and handsome form showed as usual to advantage in a crowd. Not that the supper room was crowded; without slowing her pace, Miss Steel made straight for Mr Forgan, tapped him with her fan, and demanded:

"Mr Forgan, can you give me Louisa's pendant?"

Mr Forgan turned to her considerably startled. "Pendant?" he echoed.

"Yes, you know; with garnets. Signor Yakko says you have it."

"*I* have it?" echoed Mr Forgan again. Then, as if

comprehending, he glanced to each side before stepping closer to her and saying in a confidential tone:

"I am afraid you must not believe all Signor Jacomo tells you. He is an unreliable character, and also, enjoys mocking the innocent."

"Do not speak thus of him!" retorted Miss Steele, affronted.

"I am sorry to have to. But it is my duty to warn you that Signor Jacomo has been implicated himself before now in thefts of jewellery, so in any trivial incident such as this, he naturally endeavours to cast the blame elsewhere."

"I do not know of any trivial incident," cried Miss Steele, now highly indignant. "But I will not have you call Signor Jacomo a thief. Nor a liar."

Mr Forgan held a finger to his lips. "Miss Steele, you are attracting attention."

"I do not mind that, Mr Forgan. Let the whole world hear me speak in defence of my friends."

The whole gathering, if not the world, heard her; heads turned; Miss Steele glaring defiance at Mr Forgan announced:

"I am ashamed of you, sir, for I thought you and Signor Yakko was friends, but if this is how you treat friends, calling them thieves and liars behind their backs, then I have no more to say." She swept off holding her head high, and paused half way down the room to turn and add at the top of her voice:

"What is more, that is what Louisa says *you* are, you know, Mr Forgan. A thief and a liar." As she proceeded out of the room Miss King asked some question of Mr Forgan, who answered her briefly before breaking into laughter that sounded over-loud in the shocked silence.

Miss Steele, with no thought of Mr Forgan's possible discomfiture, returned to find Signor Jacomo now in the concert room, standing with three other gentlemen by the pianoforte and looking through some sheets of music. She hailed him:

"Signor Yakko, what do you think: Mr Forgan calls you a thief and a liar."

"No doubt he has his reasons," said Signor Jacomo smiling.

"How can you say so? I declare. I was never so angry in my life. I told him that that was what Louisa said he was, even if she was raving, and perhaps after all she was not."

Signor Jacomo's companions were understandably mystified by her allusions, and looked inquiry at him. He said:

"We need not discuss this before listeners. Come," drawing her out towards the corridor, "tell me more privately what James said to you."

"Mr Forgan? I have told you what he said. And I think you might thank me, for taking your part, and standing up for you, making a show of myself in public."

"I do indeed thank you," he agreed.

"Well, I could not let him say you had done jewel robberies, after all. As if I did not know you better than that."

"I am grateful for your good opinion."

"It is not an opinion, it is a fact, and it is nothing to laugh at. If I thought you were a thief, would I think of marrying you?"

"Is that what you had thought of?" he inquired, still smiling his glint of a smile.

"Well, indeed, it was you who asked me."

"I asked you?" He seemed a little taken aback.

"Lord, do not say you have forgotten that as well. You said you would take me to your house in Milan, but not with any impropriety, and that I should be called Signora and that I was the Signora of your dreams. And that you would show me all the cities of the world, and a garden full of scented flowers. You cannot have forgotten all that?"

For a moment Luigi Jacomo almost felt tempted. She entertained him, this absurd creature; behind her ignorance he divined a quality of innocence that touched him; she had curiosity without perception, fell for the most exaggerated flattery yet sought no one's regard, and was intrepid in her enterprises and indomitable in her self-conceit; she would be easy to handle, and undemanding company. But, no, he reflected: she had no feeling at all for music. He would not have attempted to share any of his personal, musical, life with anyone, but to live with someone with whom the vital life could not be shared would prove intolerable. He had decided in that moment's reflection what he would do: he was forty-five years old and not without experience of similar situations. He laid his finger to his lips, glancing from side to side, but with a very different implication from Mr Forgan's in making the same gesture.

"I have forgotten nothing," he said in a low voice. "But this, my dream Signora, is not the time nor place to enter into such intimate colloquy. Let me tell you what is the custom in my native land: When two happy people wish to exchange pledges, they meet first in secret, in some discreet place, and speak in blessed privacy. Shall we do that?"

The idea appealed at once to Miss Steele. By now the audience was strolling in the corridor waiting for the music to recommence, and privacy was impossible. She consented with rapture to a meeting with Signor Jacomo at daybreak tomorrow, in the third embrasure of the hedge of the Spring Pavilion terrace, and, laying her finger to her lips, withdrew to force herself into listening to the rest of the concert.

Signor Jacomo meanwhile went to the singer and his accompanist, with whom he must remain professionally on good terms, and apologised for a sudden headache that compelled him to retire to bed forthwith. On his return to the Kings' house, he packed his box, wrote a note of gratitude and apology to Mrs King, and searched James Forgan's room in case of hidden money; pocketing what he found, he recognised that to be rid of James and his sordid intrigues would be a compensation for anything else left unfinished in England. Luigi Jacomo had meant to return to Milan within a few days, and was in every way ready to go. Driving away through the dark town he thought with anticipatory pleasure of his walled garden and his white cat Filippo.

At daybreak, he was awaiting the Channel packet. Soon after daybreak, Louisa was downstairs to bid farewell to Mrs Ferrars and the children. George and Augusta clung to her and begged her to come and see them in London.

"Promise you will see us again, Louisa!"

"I promise I will, as soon as I can."

Mrs Ferrars said: "Where is Nancy? It is like her, to sleep late and not to rouse herself to see us depart. Oh, well, I shall be meeting her soon enough, I do not doubt. Augusta, you have dropped your muff. George, where is your hat? Well, Louisa, we too shall meet again some time, I suppose. Tell Nancy that you should not pay for the drainpipe, it is for the owners of the house to do that. Jenny, you would do better to carry Miss Augusta's muff. We must start; I hope to be at Beckleston by midday, where we shall have a meal at the inn."

They drove off into a sudden squall of rain, and Louisa was left in a house suddenly empty. It struck her now that in promising George and Augusta to see them 'as soon as she could', she had added that modification because she had no idea of when or how she might go to London, or indeed of any plans for her future. Mrs Collier's letters had been full of inquiry after Louisa's health but did not indicate what was to become of her upon her leaving Brightsea, a departure that began to seem imminent. Louisa's grandfather, she knew, did not want her with him in Bristol. Would there be another house somewhere, another Miss Steele? Her spirits sank at the thought. On this empty wet morning, the activity of summer stilled, Louisa wished only that she could be going back to school.

When Miss Steele, after waiting through that same squall of rain and several like it, that drove through the hedge of the Spring Pavilion terrace, finally returned to

Stanley Crescent, she too felt the emptiness of the house. She had meant of course to be home before Lucy left, to amaze her, but now she was thankful that Lucy was not here to quiz her on her sodden dress and unexplained absence. For nothing else was she thankful, and certainly not for Louisa's solicitude.

"No, I am not wet through, nor am I cold. Do not stare at me like that. Why should I not take a morning walk? Leave me alone, Louisa. I am going to bed." She retired to nurse her broken heart, although as ever she could not help hoping: Signor Jacomo had been detained, he was taken ill, he would soon call and explain his failure of their tryst; all would yet be mended. The squalls ceased and the sun shone; was it merely fear of the weather that had kept him away? Musicians, perhaps, were susceptible to cold? The doorbell rang, and Miss Steele leapt out of bed to listen: from the voices below, Miss King had called to see Louisa. Presently, from her window Miss Steele saw the two of them walking off down the Crescent in the rain-washed sunshine. She almost threw up her window and called to Louisa that she must not go out, but did not; what did she care, if young girls walked happily together; what did she care if Louisa died?

About an hour later, when Louisa returning came in to ask how Miss Steele did, Miss Steele almost wished Louisa dead for the news she brought:

"... And Miss King says that Signor Jacomo is gone away, back to Milan. He left last night, without telling anyone."

"I do not believe you. Louisa, why are you gaping at me?"

"I am sorry, Miss Steele. Have you the headache?"

"No. Yes. What were you saying? Why is Signor Jacomo gone?"

"They do not know. Miss King says Mr Forgan is very sorry about it. I think it must have put him quite out of temper, because he was most unkind to Miss King this morning, and made her unhappy."

"Be quiet, Louisa. What do I care if that silly girl is unhappy?"

Louisa, since Miss King's recent disclosures suggested that her admiration of Mr Forgan had been subjected to too great a strain, was not in this context sorry either that Miss King should be unhappy, but did not expand on the topic. After a cautious offer of hartshorn or cologne, she left Miss Steele, and went down to look into the drawing-room; it was too empty; she could not settle here. She went upstairs and sat looking through her Latin notebook and regretting the lessons; there had been no suggestion since her illness that they be resumed.

Miss Steele lay all day abed, waiting to die, and at the same time planning to travel to Milan, or to write a letter that Mr Forgan could surely direct for her, or to kill herself and make Signor Jacomo sorry. This last notion, however, did not recommend itself to her. Her energies regathered into anger, which was frustrated through lack of its object; nor was she certain that, were Signor Jacomo to reappear, she could be angry with him at all. Her energies, by next morning, did not allow her the refuge of bed, and she descended to vent her anger on Louisa, as the only available victim.

It seemed to Miss Steele today that a part of her life had been wasted and that she was back where it had begun, shut up with a dull bookish girl; having lost her heart for gaieties, she felt there could be none in the world. Certainly none were proposed by Louisa's subdued mien. Yet, outside, the sun shone clearer for yesterday's storms, and the activities of Brightsea continued; September was barely here, and if there had been departures there were arrivals. Miss Steele, feeling that she would never be able to face people again, yet requiring new ribbons for the bonnet ruined in her abortive tryst, scolded Louisa out to the haberdasher's, where Louisa met Miss King.

"We have my cousin and his friend coming this week, as

soon as the Costaynes are gone," Miss King told Louisa.
"They are in the army, and I have met Charles – my
cousin's friend – already, and he is an excellent dancer, so I
hope for some diversion. The Costaynes are going to Bath,
you know, and have asked me to visit them there. I shall be
happy to go. Oh, and Mr Forgan is gone," she added with
lowered face and a tinge of a blush.

"Where did he go?"

"I do not know. To tell you the truth, I do not want to see
him again, nor do I suppose I shall, because I believe there
was some trouble with my uncle; Mr Forgan asked to
borrow money – Oh, I did not inquire. Shall I see you at the
ball next week? I shall present my cousin to you. He dances
well, if not as well as Charles – Mr Wayne, I mean. I must
not seem too familiar."

When she returned home with the ribbons, to be scolded
because they were not in a bright enough shade of purple,
Louisa did not mention to Miss Steele that Mr Forgan was
gone. No conversational overture of hers was accepted by
Miss Steele, who retired to her room slamming the door,
not to emerge again until the following morning. A letter
awaited her.

"Lord," said Miss Steele, "those ribbons you brought
look terrible, Louisa. I suppose I must force myself out for
new ones. It is a fine thing when a girl as educated as you
cannot accomplish a little simple shopping. And what does
this letter say ..." She tore it open. "It is from your Mrs
Collier," she reported, frowning at the signature. "Why
need she write to me, and bother me, instead of you?" As
she read the letter her frown deepened. "Well, here is a
pickle. No, I shall not, and I am sure you will not either."

"I shall not do what, ma'am?"

"Oh, here, read it for yourself. I do not believe in reading
other people's letters but you may save me trouble."

The letter outlined at last the preparation of plans for
Louisa's future. Mrs Collier said that a house was being
sought for this winter, in London, for Louisa, and it asked

Miss Steele whether she were free to continue there as Miss Retford's companion?

"I had understood," said Louisa, "that our association was formed only for this summer?"

"Association? Aye, you may call it that, but I have never been with anyone who associated less than you. I shall be glad to see the last of you and dare say you feel the same."

Louisa did not reply, but her spirits had sunk a little. "I do not much care for London," she ventured after a while.

Had Miss Steele been in better humour she would have seen the advantages of a house, probably as grand as this one, in London for an entire winter. All she could see at this moment was that she was tired of Louisa. She went out in search of purple ribbons while Louisa, knowing that she herself had brought the brightest shade of purple ribbon to be found in the town, decided to avoid Miss Steele's retributory wrath by walking out a little on her own. Her spirits rose at once when, in a small park behind the church, she saw Miss and Mr Dwyer strolling, possibly until time for the mid-morning service. They greeted her as kindly as usual, and she was tempted to confide in them her trepidation about her future.

"I know my grandfather is always ill, and I wish that I could spare him any worry, but I am afraid I present him with a problem. Am I to spend all my life in houses rented for me, with paid companions?"

"I do not think so," said Miss Dwyer. "You will find a settled home soon."

"I cannot see how. And, you see, now that Miss Steele has been asked to remain in charge of me, I am no happier, and evidently she is not. She has been kind to me, often, but she does not find me congenial. She says she will not come to London, but," remarked Louisa with a tone of pity that would have infuriated Miss Steele, "where else is she to go? Mrs Ferrars does not want her."

Miss and Mr Dwyer listened with sympathy but had no solution to offer to the problems presented by Louisa to her grandfather, nor by Louisa and Miss Steele to one another. However, as the church bell rang, and Louisa went to attend the service with Miss Dwyer, she felt restored for the present, and could encounter Miss Steele and her ribbons with fortitude.

This fortitude was dealt a severe blow on the next day by Miss Steele herself. She had been out to change her purple ribbons for pink, and came back to tell Louisa: "Well, it seems your kind friends the Dwyers are to abandon you. It is the same all the time, nothing but treachery –"

"You have met with the Dwyers?" Louisa interrupted, anxious.

"How else would I know they are going? You will be better without them. They are a prim pair. Yes, she says they are to go early back to where-it-may-be, because she is well, or ill, I forget which. I marvel they did not tell you themselves."

"No; they said nothing yesterday," admitted Louisa, much cast down.

"So you would not have known until they were gone," said Miss Steele with satisfaction. "Lord, clergymen are as bad as anyone. I never liked him much."

Louisa, unable to concur in such a sentiment, went up to her room to grieve and puzzle in solitude; but almost at once the doorbell rang, and Miss Steele was shrieking from below:

"Louisa, here are callers, and you must receive them, because I have not the time. Hurry. You are always hiding away when you are needed." Louisa obediently hurried down to see Miss Steele slamming herself into the dining-room while John had barely ushered the caller into the drawing-room. Entering, Louisa found that the caller was Miss Dwyer.

Restraining herself from saying immediately: But Miss Steele said you were going away, Louisa could summon no other speech. Miss Dwyer began:

"I hope I am not intruding, but we had some news this

morning that has affected our arrangements."

"Only this morning?" cried Louisa in some relief.

Miss Dwyer, a little surprised, went on to explain that her brother had heard of the illness of the friend who was acting as his locum tenens and, as Miss Dwyer was so much recovered, and the curate likely to be hard pressed, she and Mr Dwyer were to return to Staffordshire as soon as their arrangements could be altered. "We may travel next week," said Miss Dwyer, "but first, there is a plan that we very much want to be able to settle. We had intended, when we left, to ask you to come with us on a visit, and so we still intend; will we be allowing time for you to write to your grandfather for permission? I shall write too, of course. I wish you would come, Miss Retford. It is quiet in our neighbourhood, but the countryside is pleasant. You could perhaps bear me company until I am fully strong again, and Martin will have the time to continue your Latin lessons."

Louisa could have conceived of no plan more delightful. Her face as she listened to Miss Dwyer became radiant. "Oh, I shall write to my grandfather – or, Mrs Collier – at once, and how grateful I am to you. I shall love to be in the country and to help you in any way I can, and to have a little peace before I need go to London, and a rest from Miss – That is, I shall be so happy, and I do not see that permission will not be given."

"You and Miss Steele," said Miss Dwyer smiling, "may be the happier for a period apart." When, as soon as Miss Dwyer had left, Louisa ran to Miss Steele with her news, Miss Steele did not prophesy great happiness from it, at any rate to Louisa.

"So you are to go visiting," she exclaimed. "Well, I wish you joy, but there is none in making visits. One always has to be grateful and tidy and fall in with the ideas of others. And you are to go next week? Well, I shall be glad to be rid of you, but what am I to do? You have no thought of me, abandoned here for two weeks or so, with no one to talk to. I am in charge of you, and I shall write to your grandfather and forbid this visit."

"Please do not, ma'am. I am sorry to leave you, but you will have some time to rest, and there is a ball, Miss King said. Or you need not stay?"

"I do not know where I should go. Well, decide it all for yourself as of course you always do, in your stubborn way. Go off with your prim friends; you will find they tire of you soon enough."

"The visit will not in any case be long, I believe. As soon as a house in London is found, I shall expect to join you there."

For this Miss Steele was not grateful. "I dare say you will. And you will be more bookish and dull than ever."

"I am afraid you may find me so," agreed Louisa, smiling, because Miss Steele could not cloud her expectation of happiness.

Mrs Collier raised no objection to Louisa's travelling to Staffordshire; as there was some delay in obtaining a house in London, the respite could be convenient. Thus, a week later, Louisa parted from Miss Steele with a civil appearance of regret, and set out on her visit.

To anticipate: It may be imagined that everything about the visit delighted Louisa even more than she had expected. The fine modern vicarage, the countryside, and above all the company of Miss and Mr Dwyer, made her happier than she had ever been. The Dwyers too found Louisa such a welcome guest that they could not bear to lose her. After a few weeks, Louisa wrote to ask that she might extend her stay with them; presently, following another such request since she must be with the Dwyers for Advent Sunday, the renting of a London house was deferred. Then the Dwyers begged Louisa to remain for Christmas; and so it went on; and meanwhile, the affection between Mr Dwyer and his pupil was becoming manifest, which Miss Dwyer observed with satisfaction. By the spring, there was no thought of Louisa's leaving them; and when she and Mr Dwyer were married, the household continued in unabated accord. The wedding took place not much more than a year after Louisa's leaving school; looking back, she was amazed that her life had been so transformed, and herself along with it. She had written once or twice to Miss Steele on first arriving in Staffordshire, but had no answer. Louisa regretted this, since she connected Miss Steele with the summer in Brightsea that could be remembered with pleasure; it was there that Louisa's happiness had been born and that she had met with Mr Dwyer; nothing else did Louisa trouble to recall.

16

Miss Steele, abandoned in Stanley Crescent, passed some days in loneliness, dejection, and annoyance with the servants who would plague her about curtains, drainpipes and groceries. But soon, in spite of herself – or, because of her nature – she had cherished her broken heart so closely that she became fond of it. As Signor Jacomo had suspected, her imagination was not powerful except in relation to herself; she did not regret him, nor his house in Milan, but recreated them as her own attributes. She it was, Miss Steele came to recognise, who had had a proposal of marriage from a distinguished Italian gentleman with a *palazzo* in Milan and the habit of travelling to the great cities of the world. The proposal Miss Steele had, for a reason she would presently think of, refused; but her self-esteem was refreshed. She trimmed her bonnet with the pink ribbons and sallied out to walk on the promenade and to display her enhanced importance.

She had not yet considered her future in positive terms; she had decided that she was tired of Louisa, tired of acting as paid chaperone, and tired of Brightsea; none of those could be adequate to a Signora. Dawdling along in the misty sunlight she gazed ahead, like one musing on distant towers and spires; she was roused only when she saw Dr and Mrs Aylward approaching, walking with a tall and very well-looking gentleman of about thirty years of age.

Yes, admitted Mrs Aylward when Miss Steele accosted the trio, their son Dr Peter Aylward had at last arrived to visit them.

"You are come late upon the scene," Miss Steele challenged him. "We have expected you this ever so long."

With a charming smile Dr Peter Aylward answered her: "I am sorry for that."

"Could you not have come sooner?"

"My plans depended on my wife's; she was engaged to go to her father in Scotland, but it has only now become possible for him to settle on a date."

"Your wife? I see," said Miss Steele turning away. "You must excuse me. I have plans of my own to make."

In truth, she had. The disappointment had all at once given her mind a spur of action, as if she were liberated and had nothing else to wait here for. How right she had been, she told herself as she hurried back to Stanley Crescent, to become tired of Brightsea, she who could have lived in Milan.

She informed the servants: "I am leaving."

They began clamouring, to know what was to be done about them, and about tidying the house, and about the bills outstanding. Miss Steele announced that she did not care.

"Mrs Collier engaged you; apply to her. And if the solicitors want the bills, let them come and collect them. I leave tomorrow."

As she packed her boxes she reckoned up her acquisitions: many new gowns and bonnets, money in hand from her employers, freedom; she determined to go in the first instance to her cousins in Holborn. Her optimism, assured her that they would be longing to hear all she had to tell of her betrothal, her new clothes, and all the adventures of this romantic summer in Brightsea.